BEFORE THERE
WERE THE
GOSPELS,

THERE WAS . . .

THE STORY
OF JESUS
AND US

*A Love Story In
The Shadow of
The Cr*

D1607596

B.

DAVID L WETZELL, PHD

BEFORE THERE WERE THE GOSPELS,

. . . THERE WERE ORAL PERFORMANCES OF THE GOSPEL BY FOLLOWERS OF JESUS!

THE STORY OF JESUS AND US

A LOVE STORY IN THE SHADOW OF THE CROSS

. . . imagines an oral performance of the Gospel by two of the Gospel's minor characters who also tell their own unusual love story. This is a story told by Mary, sister to Martha, and Clopas, the blind beggar healed by Jesus in John 9. Together, Clopas and Mary weave into their performance of the Gospel the new reality Jesus created which allowed their relationship to flourish. Their performance of the Gospel takes place inside someone's house in Jerusalem, a couple of years after the end of the Gospel of John. It follows the general outline of the Gospel of John with parts of the Gospel of Luke interwoven within. The audience of this two person play that Mary and Clopas perform is full of people interested in following Jesus.

It includes speculations that tie together different parts of Scripture so as to provide a realistic yet faithful portrait of Jesus and the impact his life, death and resurrection had on the lives and relationships of those with him.

The Story of Jesus and Us is part Bible story, part love story, and part script for a date night! May the love from Jesus spill over into your heart as well!

David C. Wetzell

For Jesus, Mary, Clopas,

and My Family, both Biological and Spiritual . . .

"Greet Mary, who has worked very hard for us." *Romans 16:6*

"Neither this man nor his parents sinned; this came about so that God's works might be displayed in him." John 9:3

"Having loved his own who were in the world, he loved them completely. " *John 13:1b*

"And there are also many other things that Jesus did, which, if they were written one by one, I suppose not even the world itself could contain the books that would be written." *John 21:25*

"The dogma is the drama!" *Dorothy Sayers*

Note: sometimes scriptural quotations were paraphrased, based on the Holman translations.

Table of Contents

Introduction[1]

MARY AND CLOPAS: *We believe in the beginning was Jesus.*

It was Jesus in and from the beginning.

And, as all things were created through Jesus, so were our own stories.

We are here to share the story of Jesus and us, as it was created through Jesus.

For his light shone into our darknesses and made a new life for both of us possible.

We are here to testify about his light.

The light that changed our worlds.

The light that made us believe first in Jesus and second in us.

We believe that our love story bears witness to the love story.

Of how God loved us so much that God suffered, so we would believe and not perish.

CLOPAS: [gesturing to himself and Mary] But let

---

[1] based on John 1

6

us introduce ourselves. Call me
Clopas. I was born blind. My parents
had little use for me. The name they
gave me expressed their shame. I do
not even use that name now. But then
Jesus gave me sight. I would have done
anything for him. I wanted to change
my name to Cleopatros, son of a
renowned father. For in my eyes, Jesus
was my true father. But when I said
this, Jesus laughed and said that
instead of Cleopas[2] he would call me
Clopas[3], or the changing one, and both
names stuck.

Clopas was a good name for me. For I
have been changing ever since I met
Jesus, just like my wife, Mary. [glances
lovingly at her]

But before she introduces herself, let
me say that I can still remember when
I first saw her. I could not stop
looking at her. I had never seen
anyone so beautiful. As one born
blind, I was strongly drawn to her
beauty and her passion. For, as God
willed it, when we first met her eyes
were completely for Jesus, and with
good reason!

MARY: [laughing] *My husband Clopas is correct! I did*

---

[2] Luke 24:18

[3] John 19:25

fall in love with Jesus when I first met him. When I first met Clopas, I was overwhelmed with anxiety and put off by his intensity. But if I had not fallen for Jesus first, I never would have fallen for Clopas. There's something about Clopas's eyes that reflect the love of his savior. When he looks at me there's a compassion. It's so different from the eyes of many men that have looked at me over the years. But I'm getting ahead of myself.

I think we both fell for Jesus in our own ways. We both also had our hearts broken by Jesus. He broke our hearts because they had to be broken in order to be remade. And, while I did long to be the wife of Jesus, I am now adopted into his family. But that also deserves a later explanation.

CLOPAS: Yes, it does. In our presentations of the good news of Jesus, we each begin by sharing a key memory of Jesus that will show you how he remade our hearts so we could love him rightly. . . .

MARY: and come to love each other!

CLOPAS: Of course! And, our individual stories demonstrate how different we were and how important Jesus was for the creation of our marriage and how vital he is to sustaining it. Why don't you go first, Mary?

Mary and Clopas's Memories of Jesus

MARY: *My memory of Jesus comes from the intimate relationship I began with his mother shortly after I started following Jesus. Mary, the mother of Jesus, helped me to see Jesus differently, as more than a potential husband, when she shared a story about Jesus at a wedding in Cana. The wedding took place shortly after we met Jesus. At that time, Jesus was more than thirty years of age. He had worked as a carpenter since the death of his stepfather Joseph, providing for Mary and his four half brothers and his two half sisters. Because of this, many of the women thought Jesus was ripe to get married. They would do favors for Mary in hopes that she would push Jesus to marry them.*

And, what more could be expected of Mary at a wedding than to push for her first-born son to get married? But that is not what Mary did. She remembered that Jesus was not just her son. And so, she pushed him to do greater things.

And, miracle of miracles, Jesus saved the wedding by turning water into wine, but that miracle was not the heart of the story. It was just a sign. Jesus was called to bring new wine for many, not just the wine of marriage for one lucky woman. The finer wine of his glorification was meant to come. . . .

CLOPAS: Like Mary, my heart for Jesus had to be remade. But it was harder to change my heart. My heart changed with a different story. When Jesus cleansed the temple of money-changers at the end of his ministry[4], he created an image that will forever be branded in my mind.

It was the second time he had cleansed the temple, and like the first time[5], he kicked open a nest of vipers. If that first cleansing put his ministry on a sword's edge for the next three years, the second time led him to the cross. He shook up the system and challenged the way the powerful profited from piety.

I thought it was time for payback in the form of physical violence. What did Jesus do? He made a whip, but he didn't use it on the money-changers. Instead, he respected their bodies as temples. He took action against their "things," not their persons, and he spoke the truth.

"Stop turning my father's house into a market place!"[6] Jesus cried as animals yelped and their pungent odors mixed with our own. The havoc certainly subverted the holiness of the temple.

With the crackling of the whip, pouring out of coins and overturning of tables, I thought, this was it!

---

[4] **Luke 19**

[5] **John 2**

[6] **John 2:16**

Here was the zealot we'd needed for so long. He could be our zealot Messiah. He could be the one who would rally us Jews around the temple and drive out our hypocritical leaders and the Romans, so we could finally be a true nation of God and no longer slaves to the Roman Empire!

But he did not do that. Instead, he pointed away from the temple which was just a building, another material thing. Jesus pointed not to the temple but to himself. He knew the system was corrupt and that we all have been corrupted and need to be cleansed.

[Placing a hand over his heart] I was corrupted. I let my anger over the recent murder of Lazarus and my love for my country almost tear me away from Mary. [A tear forms in Mary's eye] We'd recently pledged ourselves to one another, but my enthusiasm almost ended us. For she began to fear she would lose me too, as she almost did. So I had to choose: to love my wife or to love my country, to lay down my ideals or cling to them. It began to tear me apart. But then Jesus stepped in to bring us back together.

MARY: [grasping Clopas's hand] *He helped us to see why we have to be lifted up above the passions and fears that chain us.*

Mary's Story and First Encounter with Jesus[7]

MARY: [Sighs] *I was full of fear when I first met Jesus for I was about to be stoned. My stoning was the price of my prostitution and almost the final chapter in a tragic story, not unlike the stories of how so many get swallowed by sin*[8]. [Sighs again, heavily] *Let me begin where I should . . . at the beginning of it all.*

I came from a good Jewish family: my parents, my brother Lazarus, my sister Martha and me. We were devout and once very happy. What happened? Lazarus got sick when we were young. It grew worse with time, and it was costly to keep him alive[9]. *The burden was borne by my father and mother for years, but it was too much. Eventually, my father died and my mother quickly followed, leaving us with nothing. We would have starved if it had not been for a family friend, a member*

---

[7] based on John 8

[8] Mary the wife of Clopas in John 19:25 or Mary the mother of James the younger or the other Mary in the other crucifixion/resurrection gospel accounts was either a 4th Mary or Mary the sister of Martha. The Story of Jesus and Us assumes the latter, since it continues an awesome story line, while the former seems to be mere biblical trivia. Another key speculative leap is that it is Mary the sister of Martha who was the former prostitute, not Mary Magdalene.

[9] Lazarus has Duchennes Muscular Dystrophy. This is a faster version of Beckers Muscular Dystrophy. In the mornings of this past year, David L Wetzell has taken care of a man with Muscular Dystrophy. Duchennes MD usually kills someone when they are 25. This puts Mary and Martha in their early twenties. It gives Mary eight or so years to save up the nard that was worth a year's worth of wages, which she anointed Jesus with in John 12.

of the Sanhedrin and a scholar of the Torah, who served as our "god-father" and came to our "rescue." [grimaces]

Now, I had always been very beautiful. My sister Martha was very jealous of me. Like the sisters Rachel and Leah, it stirred up a rivalry between us[10]. I began to view my beauty as my curse. Our god-father, who was supposed to be holy, [spits on the ground] introduced me to my sinful occupation. It began simply, and I knew what was happening to me was wrong, but I believed I had no choice. And he knew many others who would pay a good price for a beautiful woman in their bed.

I was ashamed. My family did not know at first. They thought the money was from our godfather, and it was true that some of it was. They blessed God and him for the provision for our need. But I could not keep my shame a secret. The burden was too great. Too much money and too much time away from our home. Martha was the first to discover me. She called the money filth and threw it on the ground. She shook me. She was disgusted. But then she looked at the money again and reconsidered. She agreed to let me continue the arrangement.

This drove a wedge between us. My brother saw both my misery and how Martha resented me. Soon, I confessed the truth to him as well. He joined me in weeping. We wept both for me and the rift I'd caused in our family. He committed himself in prayer on our behalf.

Yet for years, nothing changed and I grew depressed and haunted by my sins. In spite of this, I continued to work

---

[10] **Genesis 29-30**

in Jerusalem, away from our home in Bethany. I provided for my family, and I began to save money. Finally, it was enough for me to retire. I hoped that a good dowry would make for a good marriage. The right marriage contract would provide for my family and give me peace from my demons. It wasn't a sure thing, by any means, but I thought then that it was my only hope.

But God had other plans. When I told my god-father that I was going to retire, he was enraged. He beat me and rained curses upon my head. So I continued, but my depression only got worse, and I grew more desperate to retire. So great was my desperation that I made the mistake of threatening to expose him. Too easily he relented, begging me for just one more visit. I accepted, unknowingly walking straight into a trap.

He used my body one last time, and once we'd rearranged our robes, he dragged me onto the street. I was caught. Now, he was a married man and so the Torah forbade him to have sex with a married woman or a virgin[11]. I was neither. . . . So there was no worry of retribution for him. He and his friends crowded around me in a rough circle, ready to cast their stones. They jeered and taunted me, their eyes blazing with anger. They were forcing me to an empty field at the edge of the Jerusalem when we passed by the temple where Jesus was teaching from the Torah. Then, my god-father decided to kill two birds with one stone. . . .

He stopped and questioned Jesus about my situation, confident that the Torah was on his side. Jesus looked

---

[11] **Deuteronomy 22:22-4**

14

from me to him, and he saw the truth. He saw revenge. As such, he intuited that there would only be one real witness. But to stone someone, you need at least two witnesses. So by the law, Jesus must have had him backed into a corner[12].

Now, Jesus could have used the Torah as a sword. He could have brought the shame down that my "god-father" deserved. As with Clopas and the money-changers, I wanted judgment and punishment for my abuser. But Jesus came to teach us, not to pass judgment on us. He wanted to save me, my god-father, and those greedy money-changers in the temple.

And so, with the crowd focused on him, Jesus bent down and wrote with his finger on the ground. It took us all by surprise. [voice begins to shake] When my god-father pressed the question, Jesus stood up straight and said. . . .

CLOPAS: [picks up where her voice has trailed off] "That 'one' of you who is faultless shall throw the first stone."

MARY: He bent down and wrote again on the ground. I was full of fear and awe.

What did he write? Later, I asked him and he told me.

CLOPAS: [imitating Jesus] "It doesn't matter. What is written must be made flesh and abide among us. They were taking words written in the Torah meant to help women and using them to murder you. So much of what is written is like

_____

[12] Deuteronomy 17:6-7

15

scratchings in the sand or on stone;
when we obsess over the scratchings,
we fail to testify about the light
that gives meaning to those
scratchings."

MARY: *Then, when my god-father heard what Jesus said, he left and was soon followed by everyone else. Then Jesus and I were alone. He looked at me with those beautiful, non-calculating eyes.*

CLOPAS: [imitating Jesus] "Where are they?
Has no 'one' condemned you?"

MARY: *"No one, sir."*

CLOPAS: [imitating Jesus] "Nor do I condemn
you. You may go; do not sin again."

MARY: *Right then and there, I fell in love with Jesus. He was the answer to our prayers. However, I remained trapped. This time I was trapped by my belief that only a good husband like Jesus, could truly free me of my shame and fears and how heavy they weighed on me. I had no idea what lay in store for me as I began to follow Jesus. It was not long after that Clopas began to follow Jesus that the story of Jesus and us began.*

Clopas's Story and First Encounter with Jesus[13]

CLOPAS: My story did not begin until I met Jesus. I was blind from birth. My parents were ashamed of me. I had no choice but to beg. I begged from day one, first for love and then for money. I listened to others begging and soaked up their words. My talent with words was so great that my parents apprenticed me and paid for me to listen to readings of the Torah. I learned to use all of the hot parts of the Torah, appeals to my fellow Jews, to ask for money.

I did this, not for money. . . . I've never cared about money[14]. I did this for the love of my parents. I succeeded in begging for money . . . but not my parents' love.

So I became drunk on the power of words. Words made me more than someone begging for pity. They made me stand out from the crowd. They made me forget how small I was. I dreamed of being able to see.

I would sit among the blind and lame by the pool of Bethesda in Jerusalem and wait for the moving of the water.

---

[13] **based on John 9**

[14] **Clopas is on the Asperger's Spectrum.**

I wanted to be the first who got in after the water was stirred up by an angel. The first would recover.

Was it true? Yes, occasionally a lucky one would get healed . . . somewhat. It's hard to know for sure because the stories, once they reached your ears after being passed around to everyone in town, tended to be exaggerated. But when it did happen, perhaps it wasn't an angel, but rather their faith that healed them. I don't know, except that my faith at the pool of Bethesda was a twisted faith. For when I camped out there, all I would think about was my blindness and my own need to get into the water first. This was not good for my soul. It sowed bitterness in my heart. I was sure I deserved to be healed more than all the others around me because [with intensity] I *had the words. If only I wasn't blind, I would be somebody.* I could help my people. [holding right hand up to the sky and looking upwards] I dreamed of becoming a king's herald.

MARY: [laughing, steps forward] *Or maybe the king's minstrel, which I remember Jesus teased that this was the more appropriate role for you. . . .* [steps back]

CLOPAS: [chuckle, hands down] Yeah, my head was in the clouds. I had all sorts of dreams for my life then, but the one thing I did *not* dream of was marriage.

That part of my life was too painful. I could not fathom anyone ever loving me. . . . That was something I'd never known.

Then when Jesus opened my eyes, I thought he was going to make my dreams come true. I did not dream that he would bring down the walls of my dreams and make a way for what lay beneath. But let me step back to how Jesus first saved me.

After he saved Mary, he spoke to many people of the light[15] and won new followers[16], including Judas Iscariot. He also almost got stoned. But after Jesus and his followers hid for a while[17], they returned to the temple complex.

It was then Jesus heard my cry about our need to be consumed by zeal for the house of the Lord. He drew near me. Judas asked him, "Rabbi, who sinned, this man or his parents, that he was born blind?[18]"

MARY: [imitating Jesus] *"Neither this man nor his parents sinned."*

CLOPAS: Jesus grabbed my hands and drew

---

[15] John 8:12

[16] John 8:30

[17] John 8:59

[18] John 9:2

me to my feet,

MARY: [grabs Clopas's hands, imitating Jesus] *"So that God's works might be displayed in him. We must do the works of Him who sent me while it is day. Night is coming when no one can work. As long as I am in the world, I am the light of the world."* [19]

[Clopas and Mary stand together]

CLOPAS: Then right after that he spit on the ground, made some mud from the saliva, and spread the mud on my eyes[20].

MARY: [places hands over Clopas's eyes] *"Go, wash in the pool of Siloam"* [removes hands]

CLOPAS: Siloam was a much larger and less crowded place to wash than the pool of Bethesda since it did not claim to be miraculous.

But what was it like when he spread mud on my eyes? It's hard to describe. They burned, and I couldn't stop blinking. My mind buzzed with excitement. The fading ray of hope in my heart grew a mile wide. I still couldn't see, but I didn't care. I believed I would see. I ran toward Siloam and asked for help every minute till I got there. I washed and came

---

[19] John 9:3-5

[20] John 9:6

back seeing[21].

It was incredible. I was a new man.
All my neighbors and those who knew me
as a beggar said, "Isn't this the man
who sat begging?"

MARY: [imitating one of Clopas's neighbors] *"He's the one."*

CLOPAS: Some doubted, but I kept
saying, "I'm the one![22]"

MARY: *"How were your eyes opened?"* [a neighbor asks]

CLOPAS: "The man called Jesus made mud,
spread it on my eyes, and told me, 'Go
to Siloam and wash.' So when I went
and washed I received my sight."

MARY: *"Where is he?"* [another neighbor queries]

CLOPAS: "I don't know.[23]"

I did not know. I was awash in new
experiences and forgot about him. And,
as it was, my freedoms soon went sour
after I was taken before the
Pharisees.

[Clopas and Mary sit]

MARY: *Jerusalem was abuzz about Jesus after he gave
Clopas his sight and saved me from getting stoned in the*

---

[21] John 9:7

[22] John 9:9

[23] John 9: 10-12

temple. This was why Clopas was taken to the Pharisees. They were supposed to be our advocates but often they cared more about themselves. Jesus was a threat to their position.

CLOPAS: For he was an odd mix.

MARY: *He had the support of wealthy followers, not unlike the Sadducees, except these followers gave without any strings attached.*

CLOPAS: He was critical of the injustices of the Roman occupation, not unlike the Zealots, except he did not advocate rebellion.

MARY: *He was committed to prayer in the desert, not unlike the Essenes, except he remained committed to the rest of us.*

CLOPAS: And, not unlike the Pharisees, he explained the Torah for the rest of us, except he did not let the authorities bribe him.

MARY: *And his explanations were plain and simple, like the furniture he used to make.*

CLOPAS: Thus, his success bred envy. It also provided opportunities to gain status for those who could help spin his actions or words against him.

I also could have used my words to trap Jesus as the sick man whom he had healed at the pool of Bethesda[24] did.

---

[24] John 5

Jesus had told him to pick up his mat and walk, and he did. It was like my own healing and many others. Jesus healed us and then slipped away to avoid the crowd. Soon afterward we were interrogated by a dozen Pharisees at the local synagogue. It was almost overwhelming for me. I'd never seen so many faces or endured such detailed questioning before in my life. I see why the former lame man agreed to help them. It ended the verbal torture and to top it off, he got rewarded. I refused and was cast out of the synagogue.

My interrogation went like this. They kept asking me how I had received my sight. I wisely kept it simple: "He put mud on my eyes, I washed and I can see." After which some would denounce Jesus, saying, "This man is not from God, for he doesn't keep the Sabbath!"

MARY: *Others spoke oily. "how can a sinful man perform such signs?"*

CLOPAS: They could not agree. So again they asked, "What do you say about him, since he opened your eyes?" I kept it simple and told them he was a prophet, which they swept off the table.

Then they summoned my parents and asked, "Is this your son, the one you say was born blind? How then does he now see?"

MARY: [imitates Clopas's parents] *"We know this is our son and that he was born blind, but we don't know who opened his eyes. Ask him; he's of age. He will speak for himself."*

CLOPAS: They said this because they were common folk, just trying to keep their heads above water. They knew what was at stake. For how can one be a Jew and be banned from the synagogue? This is why they said,

MARY: [imitating parents] *"Ask him; he's of age. He will speak for himself!"*

CLOPAS: Then they let us go home.

The next day they summoned me. My parents had told me that I had to give the Pharisees what they wanted or I couldn't come home. They didn't believe in me and my dreams. I thought that maybe the Pharisees would see the truth and give me a chance to help them on my own terms but then they said:

MARY: [imitates Pharisees] *"Give praise to God. We know this man is a sinner!"*

CLOPAS: I was in shock. I couldn't believe what they were doing. I had wanted my entire life to see and now they were making me stab my own savior in the back to remain a Jew and a part of their synagogue. So I replied, "I don't know if he's a sinner. One thing I do know: I was blind and now I can see!" But that wasn't good enough.

MARY: [imitates Pharisees] *"What did he do to you? How did he open your eyes?"*

CLOPAS: Now, I'd been a beggar my entire life. I was accustomed to saying what people wanted to hear in order to survive. Now they wanted me to say what they wanted. For what, my life?

[stands and raises fists] A spark was lit inside of me and my inner zealot came out, "I already told you, and you didn't listen. Why do you want to hear it again? You don't want to become his disciples too, do you?"

I wasn't prepared for their reactions.

MARY: [Imitates Pharisees] *"You're that man's disciple, but we're Moses' disciples. We know that God has spoken to Moses. But this man--we don't know where he's from!"*

CLOPAS: And then my mind got quiet. A still, small voice brought up the words for the moment: Now that is remarkable, you don't know where he's from, yet he opened my eyes! We know that God doesn't listen to sinners, but if anyone is God-fearing and does

God's will, God listens to him. Throughout history no one has ever heard of someone opening the eyes of a person born blind. If Jesus were not from God, he would have no power.

In that moment, I knew I could not remain as I was. I too would need to find my promised land and begin again. So I accepted what was coming. When they spoke,

MARY: [imitates pharisees] *"You were born entirely in sin. Are you trying to teach us?"*

CLOPAS: Their words had no power over me. So what if I was born "entirely in sin"? Can God not redeem those born into slavery? The words I spoke remained in my mind. They shielded me as I was thrown out of the synagogue. And Jesus found me and asked:

MARY: [imitates Jesus] *"Do you believe in the Son of Man?"*

CLOPAS: I didn't care what he or his leader called himself, I had made my choice. I asked Jesus who the Son of Man was so I could believe in him. Jesus smiled and answered:

MARY: [imitates Jesus] *"You have seen him; in fact, he is the one speaking with you."*

CLOPAS: The same still, small voice that had sounded in my spirit earlier, brought forth my whispered "I believe,

Lord!" Like Abraham, I put my future in his hands.

This attracted the attention of some Pharisees who had followed me out of the synagogue. Jesus began to teach.

MARY: [imitates Jesus] *"I came into this world for judgment, in order that those who do not see will see and those who do see will become blind."*

CLOPAS: Some jeered and called out, "We aren't blind too, are we?"

MARY: [imitates Jesus] *"If you were blind, you wouldn't have sin. But now that you say, 'We see'--your sin remains."*

CLOPAS: Jesus began a message on the good shepherd. It made me see I was in the right herd. For Jesus was a good shepherd when he drew Mary and me into his flock at the same time. Though my eyes had been healed, I remained blind in other ways, stumbling around like a clumsy sheep. This made it hard for me to belong to the group of followers around Jesus. But when Mary caught my attention, I remained with Jesus and his followers. I believed my future would involve both her and Jesus. Thanks to God, they do.

How We Met²⁵

MARY: *I agree that God was at work in how we met –
in the home of the Pharisee Simon Iscariot, the father of
Judas[26]. Soon after his son began to follow Jesus, Simon
invited Jesus over. I believe Simon thought he would
monetarily support Jesus. But Simon, like his son, was not
a good man. I knew this because Simon was one of my
former clients and wanted to bribe Jesus over to his side,
his corrupt branch of the Pharisees.*

CLOPAS: But since he had cleansed the
temple, Jesus seemed to need "allies."
For what was he but a former carpenter
from Nazareth whose savings had begun
to dry up and whose Galilean followers
had had to leave to go back and work?

It was not a good situation.

One of his followers, Nathanael from
Cana of Galilee[27], had been betrothed
when he began to follow Jesus, but
Nathanael's family had little money to
give as a dowry to the family of his
betrothed. Both sides wanted Nathanael
to stop following Jesus and work. So
it was up to Jesus to provide for
Nathanael and the others who had
chosen to follow him. This seemed to
be why Jesus had accepted the
invitation from Judas' father Simon to

---

[25] based on Luke 7:36-50

[26] John 6:71, Luke 7:39-40

[27] John 21:2

stay in Jerusalem with him. But he accepted it on the condition that he could bring a friend: me.

At first they thought I was his servant. Jesus rebuked them and at dinnertime let me recline at the table on his side, a place of honor. Simon sat opposite with his son on his side. There also were some well-to-do friends of Simon at the table. It was quite something! I sat and listened to their discussion. Both Simon and Judas were well-spoken, excellent scholars of the Torah. But they, and their friends, also were quite comfortable and selfish.

Now, I am not a scholar. I cannot read, but God gave me the gift to see stories clearly. This let me see through their many complicated arguments. They, like a certain young, rich man[28], were mostly concerned with keeping their status. They did not want to let the word of God inspire them to change their lives. Jesus, by contrast, was the very meaning of change. For there he was, honoring a former blind beggar as if I were his own son. The Iscariots brought out their best. Jesus brought me. But then Mary entered the dining room and my

---

[28] **Luke 18**

life and our story began.

MARY: *I had never been in love before I met Jesus. I was full of anger toward men. I resented my father for dying and leaving the family in such a precarious financial position. I resented my brother Lazarus for his sickness and for making my father work so hard. I resented all the men who came to me, concerned only with their own gratification. I resented the man-made customs that held my fate by a string. My heart was a pit of resentment. For I could have no dreams of my wedding day – all my spare thoughts were filled with worry over whether or not I would marry at all. I saved as much money as I could. Money was my only hope. I thought that if I could keep my sin secret and save enough, I might afford a good match. But when my god-father exposed me, the truth was out, and my hopes of marriage dashed. I returned home, ruined.*

The one person that calmed me was Jesus. I had to find him, put my future in his hands, and hope that my complete devotion would make him see I'd be a good wife for him. My "love" for Jesus blinded me so that I did not even care if he were to take other wives. None of us would deserve all of him, but, of course, I would strive to be his top wife. All of my skills and my savings, stored as expensive perfume, would be his. I would find out later that my savings were dwarfed by the possessions of the many women who followed and supported Jesus[29].

Nevertheless, I did what I could to secure my future[30]. I

---

[29] Luke 8:2

[30] Luke 16:1-13

used a little bit of my savings to find where Jesus would be. It turned out he was in Bethany at the house of a former client of mine, and I went to him. I wore my best and brought him my prize possession: the alabaster vase in which I kept all my savings, my dowry. I wanted him to know that it'd all be his if I were his wife. I prayed, and when I saw him reclining and eating at the dinner table, there was no one else. Weeping, I fell before him and began to wash his feet with my tears. I had no cloth, so I wiped his feet dry with the long hair of my head. I kissed his feet and anointed them with a choice sample of my fragrant oil[31]. Like Ruth with Boaz[32], I begged him to extend his cloak of protection over me to save my family from ruin.

CLOPAS: I still remember the smell of that oil. We were given some of that same type of nard on our wedding night. [both smile at each other] When you've been a beggar your entire life, you do not get to smell much besides your own filth, so fragrance of any kind grabs your attention. It reminded me of the few times that I had been taken into the temple. Everyone at the Iscariot's table watched her pour herself out for Jesus. Her strong emotions attracted me. Yes, she was beautiful, but there was a depth to her beauty that went beyond the physical.

---

[31] Luke 7:37-38

[32] Ruth 3:9

That moment, her experience with Jesus, reminded me of washing my eyes at the pool of Siloam. When I saw my face for the first time, I witnessed the creation of a new reality, a Clopas. She too was being reborn as she baptized him and herself with tears. She became a woman who so clearly loved Jesus that I began to love her. I felt that if only I were a great man like Jesus, I would become worthy of someone like her.

Like I said before, when I was still a blind beggar, I had *never* imagined myself marrying. I had pushed down those thoughts with my dreams of the kind of success that could only be possible if I gained my sight. But when I was kicked out of the synagogue, these dreams died. But as I watched Mary adoring Jesus, they were resurrected. I wanted more than anything to be a man who could attract her or someone like her someday. My dreams grew thorny and began to torment me. They choked my ability to whole-heartedly follow Jesus and almost destroyed any chance of Mary and me becoming an "us". . . .

But I was not the only one moved by this event, both Simon and his son Judas were affected by her. Simon's face went white as he recognized Mary.

He began to speak in a low voice, as if he didn't realize he was speaking aloud.

"This man, if he were a prophet, would know who and what kind of woman this is who is touching him--she's a sinner![33]"

He looked around the table and upon seeing our faces realized he had spoken aloud. We all looked to Jesus for an answer.

MARY: *It was my worse nightmare. I could not breath, much less spare anymore tears. The gravity of what I had done sunk into my very bones. I wondered: What was I doing touching Jesus? What did I have in common with Ruth? The eyes of the men in the room, especially Clopas, scared me. Would they stone me, rape me, or both? Would Jesus be the one to cast the first stone? Tears pricked me eyes again, and I desperately sought Jesus's eyes. Jesus allowed me to look upon him, and when I saw how much he loved me, I was calmed. When I could breathe normally again, Jesus broke my gaze and turned to Simon.*

Once again, he responded in the wisest, most loving way possible. Jesus replied, "Simon, I have something to say to you." Did he know that Simon had been a client of mine? Simon must've been thinking the same thing. He went pale and whispered.

CLOPAS: [imitating Simon] "Teacher, say

---

[33] **Luke 7: 39**

it.[34]"

MARY: *And then Jesus began to tell a story. "A creditor had two debtors. One owed 50,000 dollars, and the other 5,000. Since they could not pay it back, he graciously forgave them both. So, which of them will love him more?"*

CLOPAS: [without pause, imitating Simon] "I suppose the one he forgave more."

MARY: *Jesus looked at me, smiled, and then turned back to Simon. He sighed saying, "You have judged correctly.[35]" He turned back to me, and with his next words, he knitted together the pieces of my shattered heart. "Do you see this woman?" he questioned. "I entered your house; you gave me no water for my feet, but she, with her tears, has washed my feet and wiped them with her hair. You gave me no kiss, but she hasn't stopped kissing my feet since I came in. You didn't anoint my head with olive oil, but she has anointed my feet with fragrant oil. Therefore I tell you, her many sins have been forgiven; that's why she loved much. But the one who is forgiven little loves little." And then, he said to me:*

CLOPAS: [imitating Jesus] "Your sins are forgiven.[36]"

MARY: *I believed him. I believed that there would be a way forward in life if I followed him. I did not need to marry him. God would provide, somehow. . . .*

---

[34] Luke 7:40

[35] Luke 7:41-43

[36] Luke 7:44-48

34

CLOPAS: I was new to Jesus. I knew he could work miracles, but his words made me wonder out loud, "Who is this man who even forgives sins?[37]" And I was not the only one who said it. Judas said the same thing as he looked at Mary. We were both in shock. Jesus had found a third way between rejecting and accepting her as his wife. He had elevated her by showing us that she was worthy of forgiveness. He honored her by praising her love and devotion to him. She'd always been an alluring woman, but now she was absolutely radiant.

I was naïve. How else would I have believed that I had a chance with Mary against Judas? He was handsome, wealthy, and well-educated. I was a mess. I could barely do anything but twist words together to beg. I had to start learning habits that most people learned over the course of their life.

But ideas have a way of getting a hold of me and my heart felt as though it had found someone. Someone who also had tied their life to Jesus. I vowed to God then that I would do everything I could to become worthy of her and to woo her. But then Jesus broke the spell in the room by saying to Mary,

---

[37] Luke 7:49

MARY: [imitating Jesus] *"Your faith has saved you, go in peace.*[38]*"*

CLOPAS: Jesus and I left with her, for there was murder in Simon's eyes. Mary invited us to her house in Bethany. Jesus accepted.

Shortly after, I tried to introduce myself to Mary but was interrupted as Judas ran to catch up with us, with a servant following behind him. Judas panted,

MARY: [imitating Judas] *"Master, my father has sinned against heaven and against you. I no longer want to be his son, let me come and serve you."*

CLOPAS: Jesus received him with a kiss. Judas then added,

MARY: [imitating Judas] *"My mother saw what happened. She has women friends who she thinks would like to support you."*

CLOPAS: And so with that joyous news, Jesus embraced him again and he joined us after Mary explained to Judas' servant where in Bethany we were going. Mary walked on one side of Jesus and Judas on the other. I chose to trail behind. I could see that Mary no longer had eyes only for Jesus. She also gazed upon Judas who was everything I am not . . . thank God!

---

[38] Luke 7:50

[Mary and Clopas laugh.]

MARY: *For me, it was like I was falling in love with Jesus again, but this love was different. I felt free from fate and the entanglements of my gender. He'd shown me that I was free to give back to him the same love that he gave to me, the very love of God. I wanted to know more of what Jesus taught.*

And, my thoughts were far from Clopas. Anticipation flowed like honeyed wine through my veins. For the first time in a long time I was happy and full of hope for what was to come. And I never would have expected what came next. Clopas turned his attentions toward me, and his "tactics" had the very opposite effect of his intent! He had no idea how to turn a woman's head, and I tried to avoid him as much as possible! [Mary rolls her eyes and shakes her head. Clopas laughs.]

Clopas's Big Mistake

MARY: *After the journey from the Iscariots, we arrived at my home long after the sun had set. Martha's face was squeezed into a tight frown, but she would not express her anger with me over my disappearance in front of the men. Her anger quickly gave way to shock over the company I'd brought into our home. When I introduced them she asked, "So this is your savior?" She was quickly fascinated with Jesus, for she too was looking for a savior to save her. She believed she was due. She had always been good and faithful to the Law, unlike me. So the next morning she woke up early to clean and prepare a large meal for our guests and Lazarus. She let me help some, but when it came time to serve, she made it clear who was responsible.*

Jesus and the others ate well. Judas praised Martha so eloquently that it made me jealous. Clopas sat to the side and said little, but he would sometimes gaze at me so intensely that it caused me to squirm. I tried to ignore him and focus my energy on Jesus, Judas, and Lazarus. My brother was in awe of Jesus, and it was so good to see Lazarus excited. As the day waned, Martha and I told them our family's sad story.

CLOPAS: Not all sad, my dear. Don't forget that you and Martha learned how to read when your parents used some of their means and connections to get a tutor for Lazarus, before his illness progressed and they had a bit more money to spare.

MARY: *Yes, Jesus seemed especially pleased when I shared that part of the story. It was one of the blessings to come from Lazarus's illness.*

[Someone in the crowd calls out a question.]

What's that? Why didn't Jesus heal Lazarus? Well that morning we wondered the same question as we retold how long and hard we had prayed for Lazarus. We told Jesus he was a little older than Martha and me, but we had taken care of him for a long time, since he had been set apart from a young age. When he was around six years old, his legs grew weak. He had a hard time running and jumping and often fell. In a matter of years, he began to have a difficult time using his other limbs, and his arms and hands grew weak as well. He sustained plenty of wounds on his body. Eventually, he lost the ability to walk so we had to carry him, and in recent years, feed him.

Martha and I had worked together to help him for a long time. We had also given generous sacrifices at the temple in his honor. With anticipation, my family and I waited to see what Jesus would do. Jesus commented that some things take a lot of prayer and are meant to point to the glory of God.

CLOPAS: I told the others that Jesus had said the same thing to me right before he opened my eyes and gave me my sight. The miracle occurred so that God's work could be seen through me.[39]

MARY: *Jesus added that some wounds also point to the*

---

[39] John 9:3

power of God. He told us that our brokenness could lead us and others to God. Then he paused, looked at Cazarus, and asked if he wanted to be healed. There was silence as Cazarus thought about what Jesus had said.

CLOPAS: [imitating Lazarus] "Not yet."

MARY: *Martha gasped, and I could not believe my ears. How could Cazarus deliberately choose to keep our family in bondage? I later learned that he did not want his healing to attract others. He wanted us to make the most of our time with Jesus. But that wasn't the whole truth. Cazarus had a strange gleam in his eye. It was as if a silent message had passed from Jesus to Cazarus. Cazarus seemed to understand that he would serve a higher purpose later.*

CLOPAS: I couldn't understand it. I thought to be healed and set free were the most important things for anyone. I said as much. Jesus laughed and promised me that I would someday have my eyes cleared again so I could see. I didn't know what he meant by that. I was confused by a lot of things Jesus said and did, and I was so driven to succeed as a follower of Jesus. At first, I thought I wanted to be an apostle. I wanted to be somebody more important after spending most of my life as a nobody. Later, I would memorize and recite from the Psalms for everyone.

MARY: *He would do this sometimes without asking*

first . . . and instead of making sure he was ritually clean for Sabbath.

CLOPAS: My goal was to let my light shine so brightly that my weaknesses would be overlooked, but my light showcased my faults rather than my gifts. And, Jesus did not need a thirteenth apostle. He did not need a seventy-first disciple. Whereas, I needed help very much.

MARY: *Clopas could be too intense. As we sat in my home with Jesus, we had just finished telling my family's story when Clopas erupted into a rapid telling of the story of how Jesus healed him. He got so caught up in it, he could not see the rest of us. It was a bit funny, but mostly sad. When he finished his story, Clopas began to revisit what happened last night, so Jesus quietly spoke to him saying, "Clopas, I too have something to share."*

CLOPAS: I stopped and apologized. Then Jesus began with his story. His mother was also named Mary. She gave birth to him while she was still a virgin. It was a miracle birth, not unlike the birth of Sarah with Isaac, or Hannah with Samuel. The rest of the town believed she had sinned. He'd been torn by insults to his mother in his early life. His step-father Joseph had married Mary after a dream about Jesus. He was born in Bethlehem where they had gone to be counted for a census. It was a hard trip and to make matters worse their kin had no room for them, due to Mary's *sin*. So he was born in a stable, where his birth was greeted by local shepherds. Around a year later, magi from the east came to visit him.

Shortly after, his father took his family to Egypt because king Herod wanted to massacre all male children in and around Bethlehem who were two years and younger. Now, the magi had given his family some gold. Joseph tried to use it to get money for the journey and back. But the money changers looked at his simple garb and gave him outrageously low prices. And, because they desperately needed the money, Joseph took it.

MARY: *Then, while they were on their way to Egypt, they were robbed. To survive they became deeply indebted to an Egyptian merchant who "saved" them.*

CLOPAS: Thus, they, like the ancient Israelites, became "slaves." Although, Jesus reminded us that their situation was not uncommon for foreigners in a foreign land anywhere.

MARY: *Even though Joseph and Mary worked terribly hard in Egypt, their debt was so great that they had little money for food and Jesus almost starved to death.*

But then a miracle saved him from starvation. At the beginning, he behaved like a starving child. But when his suffering was at its worst, the power of God began to show itself within him. God gave him an extra inner source of energy that sustained him and freed him to accept what milk and food were given to him. He didn't waste his energy on crying or demanding more when there was none. He trusted that there'd be enough for him. Instead, he seemed to sense the weariness and hunger of others around him and was always doing his best to bring joy to others' difficult lives.

CLOPAS: How could a child bring joy . . . by finding joy that was hidden from grownups! Jesus found joy in the small things of creation like the emergence of plants and trees, the growth and life of small and large animals.

MARY: He found joy in the stumbling process of learning to walk, talk, and the use of his hands. He loved to watch his parents work hard for him, and especially he loved to listen to his parents tell him and each other stories of the ancient Israelites time in Egypt. His parents found sustenance and hope in telling what they could remember of these stories, of how God had used Moses to free the Israelites so they could become a light to all nations.

CLOPAS: Jesus commented that in this, his mother observed that he was not unlike her other children or anyone's children. But Jesus was more conscious in his enjoyment of all life's developmental stages, including his own. Unlike others, his joy was sustained and grew even more due to both the intensity of hardship and the mysterious inner energy provided by God.

Then, within a year, Herod had died and, at first, Joseph wanted to demand that his master let his family go. But then he had another dream that warned him to bide his time. Soon their master also had a dream that led him to free them and to provide for their return to Israel. Joseph took them to Nazareth in Galilee, because he did not trust Archelaus, Herod's successor[40].

"Life in Nazareth was also hard, since Joseph's health never fully recovered from their time in Egypt and he had to begin his trade again. But young Jesus made their life there bearable with his helpfulness and amazing recall of all the stories and experiences they had shared in Egypt. Thus, he, as his mother liked to put it, "increased in wisdom and stature and in favor with God and with people"[41].

Jesus laughed a little about his increase in stature, since he was shorter than most people, including

[40] Matthew 2:22

[41] Luke 2:52

44

me. He added that he believed it was because of malnutrition during the early part of his life that he was shorter. It was obvious to him that generations who grew up in hard times, as there had been plenty of in recent history, were shorter than generations who grew up in better times.

I was amazed and felt that Jesus was like me. He also had to suffer for no good reason from an early age. When he had seen me, born blind, he saw a sorrow we had shared. His suffering had also come about so that God's works might be displayed in him.

MARY: *Joseph had to work hard in Nazareth to provide for his family. For soon Mary had their own children: James, Joseph (who later renamed himself Joses), Salome, Judas, Simon and Elizabeth[42]. The hard work continued to take a toll on Joseph so he died when he was around the same age as Jesus was when we met him; over thirty, back when Jesus was around fourteen. Joseph had just trained Jesus as a carpenter so Jesus was thrust into the role of provider for his mother and their family. Jesus worked for more than fifteen years as a carpenter before he began his ministry.*

I was touched by how Jesus lost a parent due to hard times. I yearned to be a man who could learn a trade like carpentry. If only, I too had been able to take care of my family in an honest, productive way!

---

[42] **Mark 6:3**

CLOPAS: We spent the rest of the morning telling stories. Judas told us about his studies and his family. He had studied so many things. He even learned how to use a sword! It was foreign to the lives of the rest of us. It felt like his decision to come follow Jesus against the will of his father was the first time in life he had ever taken any risks.

MARY: I was impressed by Judas. The man glowed in security. I was sure then that he would become Jesus's top disciple and apostle and maybe eventually succeed him. Martha felt the same way but Judas never expressed any real interest in her, which made things worse between us.

The day went by very quickly. Soon we were eating dinner when John appeared, along with a new guest, Mary Magdalene. They had learned where Jesus was from the house of Simon Iscariot. John had brought Mary to Jesus because she had decided to sponsor him and his ministry. John's mother also wanted to monetarily support and follow Jesus[43]. They had begun their support by helping Nathanael remain an apostle. They made a generous contribution to the dowry for Nathanael to get married. It was enough so that Nathanael's wedding would soon take place in Cana. As we've already mentioned, Jesus and his disciples were invited to come to the wedding. John had to leave early the next morning to tend his family's business so he invited Jesus to come with him. Jesus wasn't sure. He wanted first to hear from

---

[43] Matthew 27:56

Mary Magdalene.

Mary Magdalene was a wealthy widow from Capernaum. Jesus had cast several demons out of her, and ever since she had kept her eye on his ministry[44]. When his followers returned home to work without him, she found out why and saw her opportunity to help Jesus. Mary Magdalene brought with her the joy that God would provide. Jesus never would need the money of Simon Iscariot.

I was fascinated by Mary Magdalene's spirit. She had been through so much. It was like she had become a stream of living water, and she knew it. This is why she trusted Jesus so much. After telling the story of how Jesus saved her, she asked to hear others' stories. She also wanted to hear about what had happened at Simon Iscariot's house. Clopas told his story—more slowly this time. Then Jesus spoke of Simon Iscariot.

CLOPAS: Jesus described briefly how my Mary had shown him great love. Jesus knew that when Simon insulted her, it was time to turn away from him.

I became fascinated with how Jesus told stories. His stories showed how much he had studied the Torah. He boiled the teachings of the Torah down but kept their flavor.

MARY: *Jesus was overwhelmed with joy that Judas had decided to follow him rather than his father. Judas spoke of his mother's desire to connect Jesus with more women to*

---

[44] Luke 8:2

support Jesus and his disciples with their possessions and care.

CLOPAS: Mary Magdalene saw that she could help. She suggested that she could meet with other women interested in supporting Jesus while Jesus went to the wedding. Mary and Judas would talk with them, along with Mary and me. Jesus liked the idea and decided that Mary Magdalene should be the head of his supporters. But Judas asked,

MARY: [sarcastically in a lower voice] *"How are you going to find men to support you if these men have to submit to a woman?"*

CLOPAS: Jesus looked at him and said with a smile,

MARY: [imitates Jesus] *"Well, with men this is impossible, but with God all things are possible!" And that was why all of Jesus's supporters were women.*

CLOPAS: And God did provide.

Mary Magdalene assured Judas that he could be in charge of the common purse, which quieted him. It also made sense. He was well educated and experienced with managing money. Later, when we approached possible women supporters of Jesus, Judas gave his word that he would manage their gifts well.

MARY: *But Judas "managed" the common purse by*

48

stealing from it. Judas never got used to the simple life of Jesus. I know this because I received some luxurious gifts from him; he otherwise could have never afforded an extravagance like white raisins. He gave these to me later on when I'd joined Jesus and Judas in their journeys, in part to create space between Clopas and I.

CLOPAS: I didn't like Judas. At first, it was because Mary preferred his company over mine. But he just seemed too perfect, too well spoken, too handsome, and too gifted. It felt as though he hid behind these things. He didn't seem to have the sort of passion that Peter had, and he wanted to succeed to be the best, so much so that he was afraid to take chances. Me, I had almost nothing *but* Chutzpah. I kept trying to get Mary to notice me, but the words all came out wrong when I needed them.

MARY: *Soon, it was settled that Mary Magdalene, Judas, Clopas, and I would meet with the possible supporters of Jesus in the coming week, while Jesus returned home with John to attend the wedding.*

CLOPAS: Jesus left the next morning. Judas and Mary Magdalene left soon afterward to meet his mother about the possible supporters. Finally, I had a chance to really introduce myself to Mary. I said hello. I told her I was glad Jesus could go to that wedding but that I'd never been to one myself.

Then I made the mistake of asking
suggestively, "Someday it'd be great
to go to one together. Don't you
agree?"

MARY: *I felt so awkward at his obvious display of affection. Clopas's face was so hopeful, it was clear to anyone with eyes in their head that he'd developed an attachment to me. I couldn't help but laugh a little, and so I excused myself so as not to be rude. My sister Martha saw the whole thing and couldn't help teasing Clopas.*

CLOPAS: [as Martha] "Why Mary loves
weddings, more than anything else. Too
bad you two couldn't go with them. I'm
sure Mary would have enjoyed getting
to know you better there." I was blind
to Martha's joke. "Really?" I asked.
She replied, "Of course! Mary is
sometimes shy. You should ask her more
about what sort of wedding she wants
to have someday. I'm sure she'd love
to tell you." I sought Mary out,
interrupting her privacy though she'd
just left the room. As she attempted
to get past me to leave a second time,
we bumped into each other
accidentally. For a brief moment, my
hands lingered at her waist, our faces
close to one another's. Blind to my
impropriety, I began to ask her
Martha's wedding question. It took me
a couple of seconds to see the

stricken look on Mary's face. I tried
to murmur an apology, but it was too
late.

MARY: *I was angry. Any mention of marriage,
especially my marriage, set me off back then . . . I thought
he must have presumed he could disregard my privacy
and touch me because I'd been a prostitute. I asked him
not to speak with me again. I know now that it was an
accident, and that I overreacted. But, nevertheless the
rest of that day and the next were full of awkward
tension. Clopas, to his credit, did try not to speak with
me again, but the intensity of his eyes spoke volumes.
Even Lazarus sensed the tension.*

*Finally, Judas and Mary Magdelene returned in the
evening, and I was glad. Martha began preparing a
wonderful meal for Judas, who excused himself to go and
exchange some jewelry his mother had given him.*

CLOPAS: Martha gave Mary and me the
duty to prepare lentil stew and bread
together. I was eager to help because
I wanted to get a chance to spend time
with Mary. But I'd never prepared stew
or bread before and was full of fear
about how to do it.

MARY: *Clopas's eagerness blinded him to another of
Martha's slights. She'd asked him to help cook, normally
a woman's or a servant's job. Martha busied herself so I
could not express my anger with her. I hated that she was
playing matchmaker! I took my anger out on poor
Clopas. He obviously had no idea about how to prepare
lentils. After a few minutes, I had to take over, or our*

dinner would've been ruined! I was so irritated that I remarked, "The only way you could make a meal appear here is if you begged for it!" Mary Magdalene, overhearing this, gently offered to take Clopas's place in the kitchen.

CLOPAS: I went outside and sat on the street not far from some beggars. I watched them ply our trade. I listened to their words. Their words were so weak, just like my hands.

I looked at my hands. Jesus had helped me to clean them before the meal at Simon Iscariot's house. I remembered how long and dirty my nails had been. I closed my fingers together and opened them again. This tiny miracle of how these tools obeyed me both amazed me and filled me with shame. I did not know how to use them. What had I used them for besides eating, swatting at flies, and clutching at whatever was thrown my way? Would I ever hold a woman as my wife and become one with her?

I sat there until Mary Magdalene came and told me it was time to eat. It was the worst meal I have ever endured. Judas dominated the conversation with his knowledge of the Torah. He held the interest of Mary, Martha, Mary Magdalene, and Lazarus, while I picked at my food, jealous of his ease and confidence.

MARY: *I don't remember exactly what Judas spoke about, but I do remember being intrigued with him. The next day it was time to prepare for our meetings with potential supporters of Jesus. We each were to practice telling our stories of how Jesus had changed us. Judas volunteered to help me, while Mary Magdalene helped Clopas to prepare his story, and Martha kept busy by taking care of Lazarus. Judas listened to my story, apologized for his father, and expressed his amazement at the legal genius of Jesus and how his simple question ended the matter.*

CLOPAS: [imitating Judas] "Let the one who is without sin throw the first stone!" It was brilliant! For even if that one were in accord with the letter of the law, they would still be shamed for the act. And there's no doubt they forgot they needed multiple "witnesses" to participate in the stoning, and so their stories would likely be inconsistent and easy to pick apart. So they let the matter go, as they should have!

"The Mosaic law was meant to extend protections to more females, initially virgins in addition to married women. It was not meant to consign unmarried, non-virgin women to a permanent under-class status. They were twisting the law to get what they wanted, totally the opposite of its original intent!"

MARY: *Judas made some suggestions, like the use of actions and vocal inflections to convey the deeper legality that Jesus hinted at.*

CLOPAS: "Let the audience put two and two together, it'll sink deeper into them then. . . ."

MARY: *I know that in the end, Judas betrayed Jesus and twisted the law for his own purposes, but I believe that in the beginning, he wished to turn away from the path of his father. He also seemed genuinely interested in me. He didn't judge me for my past. It was clear to him that I was a victim of my god-father who took my virginity and advantage of my family's tragic situation. It was that early Judas who I began to fall in love with.*

The next day, after breakfast, Judas led Mary Magdalene, Clopas, and me to visit the first potential supporter of Jesus. She was Abigail, the wife of my "god-father." I do not think she recognized me, but I was very anxious. Fortunately, Mary Magdalene began, explaining how much Jesus meant to her, and how she planned to provide monetary support for him and his followers so they would not need to take any more breaks to work and earn money. Then, Judas spoke briefly about how he was going to manage the money collected for Jesus and his followers. Then, it was Clopas's turn, to be followed by me.

CLOPAS: I began my story. I had worked on it with the help of Mary Magdalene. She encouraged me. It's easy to get caught up in one's weaknesses and to forget one's gifts. I worked on it, in part because it took my mind off of Mary, but I wanted to impress her as well.

Why was I still trying to impress Mary? I couldn't get over the memory of when I first met her. I knew I had messed up, but I believed that if I only had a chance to redeem myself that things could work out. So I thought the way forward was to put out what I thought was my best side. I would also show Judas that I too could hold forth with my own ideas. So I worked without dinner both to avoid Judas and to put together why I was a follower of Jesus. This was my time to shine.

I began my story, close to how I tell it now. I'm sure Judas recognized, [voice changes] *"Rabbi, who sinned, this man or his parents, that he was born blind?"*[45] They liked it, except for Judas. When I saw Mary's eyes start to light up, I got excited, perhaps too excited. I easily got excited, especially when I thought my actions might change Mary's mind about me. My story began to take on a zealot's fervor. I told them Jesus would remove our blind acceptance of Roman rule so that the Jewish people

[45] **John 9:2**

could be the light for all nations as we were meant to be. This upset Abigail and the others.

MARY: *It angered Judas greatly. He took charge, barking at Clopas to stop. Abigail was shaken. I bet she was thinking that her husband was right about Jesus, so thankfully, we left. Clopas had saved me from having to tell my story to the wife of my "god-father." But he had also given me another reason to dislike him, for my family had long opposed zealotry.*

When we finished with our presentations for the day, Judas demanded that we exclude Clopas from Jesus's followers. Judas claimed Clopas was wrong and dangerous to have counted in our numbers. I immediately agreed with him, though for somewhat of the wrong reasons.

CLOPAS: I was shocked that they would dishonor me so. I was also surprised to see them rebel against Mary Magdalene, the leader of our group. It fell to her to reassert her leadership and decide my fate. I naively had thought other followers of Jesus would agree with me and began to realize what a mess I had made. So I waited for Mary Magdalene to see what she would do.

MARY: *She was a fount of wisdom and grace. "Judas, we will let Jesus decide this matter. Clopas, like you and Mary, is a new follower of Jesus. He can make a mistake, just as you have by demanding his exclusion from us. The*

*truth is that his mistake is not an unusual one. It is
serious, but not unusual. We will not let him speak at the
next meeting, and we will wait for Jesus to decide, after
Clopas has had time to reflect upon his mistake. Clopas,
you need to think about the consequences of what you
just said. We followers of Jesus are not zealots! I do not
support rebellion or murder!"*

CLOPAS: So at the house of the next
possible supporter of Jesus, I waited
outside, like a servant. I hadn't
expected that the fruits of my efforts
would be so bitter. My life had been
simple up until then. I listened,
found the right words to beg with, and
hoped to earn a coin or two. Then I
would do it again. I lived in complete
autonomy. Now, as a follower of Jesus,
I was not sure how to be a member of
their group. I didn't know where I fit
in with them, and I did not know how
to discover my place. So, I let my
anger with Judas simmer and stew
within me.

MARY: *For this next visit, we met Salome who would
become a supporter of Jesus[46]. Mary began again,
followed by Judas and then it was my turn to tell my
story. I was so nervous to be speaking in front of Judas,
that I spent more time describing how I was forced to
become a prostitute, sure to emphasize how much I'd
hated it. I wanted to prevent him from rejecting me as a*

---

[46] **Mark 15:40**

potential wife. That was more important for me than pointing to what Jesus had done for me.

When I came to the point in my story where I was almost stoned, my emotions got the better of me, and the tears that fell down my cheeks turned into racking sobs. I was so ashamed, both of my past and that I had failed so badly in front of Judas. Mary came and held me right there. Despite what I felt was my failure, Salome was moved and agreed to support Jesus. But I was a mess. Just like Clopas, I was not ready to share my story with possible supporters of Jesus.

Fortunately, we returned home, where Martha had a meal waiting and Lazarus was eager to hear about what happened.

CLOPAS: There was a long silence.

MARY: *Finally, Mary gave the word, drawing on the words of Jesus. "It was a learning experience. By the grace of God, we gained a supporter for Jesus. We also gained insight. Insight into how we must not judge each other. We must learn to love each other when we make mistakes or when we bump into each other because of how we are different. We must still learn from Jesus about how to pray for those who normally would be our enemies."*

CLOPAS: But when Judas added, "We also must learn our places," I lost my temper. "It was too easy for you to say I should be cast out of Jesus's followers," I shouted at him. "If you left, you could run back home. You could live your life of comfort and respect. I don't have anything else. I was cast out of my synagogue. I am no longer a Jew. I don't know what I am, but I am nothing without Jesus.

"And yes, I am sick and tired of this world. I look forward to when it will all be brought down to its knees. I believe Jesus is the one who could do it. He could get many like me who'd be willing to sacrifice their lives for him! What about you? Would you do that? I don't think so." Judas tried to stop me, but I kept up my rant.

"I don't care what you say or how many wealthy donors you bring in to support Jesus. You are just like your father, and *you* are the one who should be cast out from following Jesus, not me. We don't need you. Jesus doesn't need you, so you can take your education, your good looks, and your fancy manners straight to Sheol!!"

MARY: *Judas turned bright red. He was set to respond in kind, but right then, Jesus's mother arrived. She requested us to come join Jesus at Cana where he'd return in a couple of days. She'd distracted us with her news, and this dispelled the drama and all of our energy. We retired to rest for the early trip the next morning.*

CLOPAS: I slept next to Lazarus, far from Judas.

Jesus's Gift to Clopas of a Second Chance

MARY: *In the morning, Martha had an early breakfast prepared. Clopas sat away from the rest of us in a corner I could tell he hadn't slept well that night. His eyes met mine in a glassy stare.*

CLOPAS: Mary and Mary Magdalene both sat next to Jesus's mother. Judas was close to Mary and Martha.

MARY: *Jesus's mother told us about the wedding in Cana. Both sides of the family were at first hostile to Jesus and his disciples. They didn't have much money for the wedding and blamed Jesus for Nathanael's lack of income. But Nathanael's bride loved him. She still wanted to marry him, even without the security of an income. When Jesus elevated the wedding's mood with his miracle, the families forgot their hostility. The father of the bride was so thankful to Jesus that he let him borrow his boat for a week the day after the wedding. So Jesus left with his disciples to escape the crowds. For many others, as you might imagine, wanted their own "water into wine" miracle.*

But before Jesus had left, he'd asked his mother to go and get us for him. He wanted to talk with us. This puzzled me, since I had no idea why he'd want to talk with both Clopas and me. What did we have to do with each other? His fascination with me, combined with my anxieties about marriage, had made me so uncomfortable that the sooner Clopas was out of my life the better!

So Judas said he'd stay and finish meeting with other

possible supporters of Jesus. Mary Magdalene agreed. Martha was overjoyed at the idea of spending time with Judas, but soon Judas' mask of politeness made it clear that he was not interested in her or even Lazarus that much.

CLOPAS: I listened from across the room. I never thought I would be afraid to see Jesus. Would he also reject me, as I was rejected by Judas and Mary? What had I done? What would come from what I said to Judas last night? I'd made an enemy. I had never had a real enemy before. I wondered how I could be enemies with another follower of Jesus. I'd fully meant what I had said, even if most of it sprang from jealousy.

So I went with them because I had no choice. When Mary became Jesus's mother's shadow, Mary Magdalene walked in silence with me.

MARY: Jesus's mother Mary and I held hands. She let me tell her my story and wept over my misfortune. Then she cried a little more over how her son had saved me. I told her I'd fallen in love with Jesus and wanted to be his wife. But instead I'd been blessed by him with a love that did not require marriage. Mary told me more about Jesus as a boy and why she did not push for Jesus to marry at Nathanael's wedding. Then she asked about Clopas. I told her what happened: how he had made me uncomfortable, spoken rashly about Jesus and brazenly *with Judas.*

[Mary sighed.] *"So Clopas thinks Jesus is going to be a Zealot leader? I thought the same when I first learned of him. I wrote a song where I sang, 'He has toppled the mighty from their thrones and exalted the lowly. He has satisfied the hungry with good things and sent the rich away empty.'"*[47] *She sighed again and admitted that she did not understand her son. "He could be anything. God is with him." But she was torn with all sorts of memories, emotions, hopes, and fears. She said, "I do not know what is to become of him, but I know we need him. Our family needs him, we're falling apart without him."*

CLOPAS: We arrived in Cana late on Friday night. Jesus's mother brought us to the place where Jesus had stayed. We were exhausted and fell asleep soon. Then word came early in the morning that Jesus was surrounded.

The news of how he had turned water into wine had spread like wildfire. The news promising Jesus's return in a week, brought many waiting for him early in the Sabbath morning when he arrived.

MARY: *It was most unusual. Jesus stood in the center of the town. On both sides of him were two important men. By their garb we could tell that one was a royal official*[48]

---

[47] Luke 1:52-53

[48] John 4:46-53

and the other a synagogue leader[49]. But both men were stricken. We asked others what was going on. They both had children who were close to dying. They both wanted Jesus to come in that moment to save their child. The crowd was all around, waiting to see who Jesus would choose to help.

CLOPAS: It was a problem worthy of Solomon, except there was no way to cut the baby in half. To do nothing was to let both children die, to save one was to make a powerful enemy. But there was no right way to choose between them, especially if one preached the need to love one's enemies, as Jesus did, for each had an equal need.

The royal official, Chuza, who was Herod's steward, presented his case. His son was ill at Capernaum. When he had heard Jesus had come back to Galilee, he came right away to find him. His son was so sick that without a miracle from Jesus, he would die.

MARY: Then, the head of the synagogue, Jairus, fell to Jesus's feet and pleaded for him to come to his nearby home. His only child, his daughter, the delight of his life, was dying.

CLOPAS: Chuza quickly added that his son was also his only child. Both glared at the other and left unspoken

[49] Luke 8:40-56

the consequences if Jesus were to choose the other.

Jesus laughed to himself and declared,

MARY: [imitating Jesus] *"Unless you people see signs and wonders, you will not believe."*

CLOPAS: Then Chuza said to Jesus, "Sir, come down before my boy dies!" Jesus lifted Jairus from the ground. He turned to face Chuza and said,

MARY: [imitating Jesus] *"Go, your son will live."*

CLOPAS: Chuza must have heard about how Jesus had cured the slave of a centurion back in Capernaum with a word[50], because he accepted it and departed. Jesus then signaled to Jairus to lead him.

MARY: *Clopas ran to catch up to Jesus. Mary Magdalene, Jesus's mother, and I sat in wonder. "Go, your son will live." What a beautifully simple phrase! How could Jesus do this? Here was one greater than Solomon, who would have had to flip a coin. I could not stop thinking, "What sort of man is this? Who could promise that a child would live and be believed?"*

Later, I found out from Joanna, Chuza's wife that Chuza and his entire household had become believers upon learning that her son was healed at the exact time that Jesus promised, "your son will live." Joanna, with her husband's blessing, became a supporter and follower of

---

[50] Luke 7:1-10

64

Jesus and a friend of mine[51]. But initially there were doubts. What if Jesus was wrong? What if the official's son dies? Could it be the beginning of the end for Jesus? There'd been no shortage of men who sold themselves as messiahs. The times were bad enough that people were as desperate for a messiah as I had been desperate for a husband. But all of these pretenders stumbled and usually died, along with many of their followers. Was the same thing going to happen to Jesus and us?

I told Mary Magdalene and Jesus's mother that I had to go and be with Jesus. It's what I came for, and I could sense the gravity of the occasion. If Jesus saved the child of the local synagogue leader then that would change things for good. But Jesus was surrounded by a crowd that seemed to grow by the minute. That was enough to discourage the other two from joining me. As it was, I could barely follow from the back, but it was definitely worth it.

CLOPAS: Normally, for a former blind man, the crowd would have been overwhelming. But I was determined and when I set my mind to something, there's little that can stop me,

MARY: [laughs] Which sometimes is a mixed blessing. . . .

CLOPAS: [laughs] Soon, I was right next to Jesus. He greeted me and then scanned the crowd to look for Mary.

---

[51] Luke 8:3

MARY: *His eyes found mine, and he smiled, greeting me by name before continuing on with Jairus. . . .*

CLOPAS: who was getting more anxious by the minute. Unlike him, Jesus was calm, even though it was not easy to move forward. We were almost crushed by people coming at us from all directions. Now, I also knew that zealot leaders often get assassinated. So I appointed myself to be on the lookout for unusual people approaching Jesus.

Because of this, I saw a woman draw close to him. She was like a living corpse. It was unusual, but obviously not a threat to Jesus's safety. However, right then Jesus stopped and Jairus' face turned bright red. I almost laughed.

MARY: *The whole crowd stopped. It was so unexpected. We all stared at Jesus who said,*

CLOPAS: [imitating Jesus] "Who touched me?"

MARY: *We all wondered what he meant by that, assuming he was angry that someone reached into his private space.*

CLOPAS: Everyone nearby denied touching him, which was, of course ridiculous since he was surrounded on all sides. But it showed how people already revered Jesus as king. One moment they couldn't get close enough to him, the

next they presumed he held their life
by a thread and might end it on a
whim. Soon Peter and others told
Jesus, "Master, the crowds are hemming
you in and pressing against you and
you ask, 'Who touched you?'"

MARY: [imitating Jesus] *"Someone did touch me. I
know that power has gone out from me."*

CLOPAS: At this point, I caught the eye
of the woman, Susanna. She was the
only other person who wasn't confused.
I cried, "There she is, Jesus. She
touched you!"

Everyone else stepped away from Jesus,
wondering what he would do. Susanna
turned white. She came trembling and
fell down before Jesus. In the
presence of all of us, she
cried. . . .

MARY: [imitating Susanna] *"Master, I have suffered
from terrible bleeding for twelve years. I have seen
doctors who have done all sorts of things to me, none of
which has worked. I've paid a lot of money to get better,
but nothing has worked. You were my last hope. That is
why I approached from behind and touched the tassel of
your robe. The moment I did that, I felt the bleeding stop
within me."*

CLOPAS: All, including the synagogue
leader, were silent as we paused to
reflect on her act of faith. Jesus
smiled and said . . .

MARY: [imitating Jesus] *"Daughter, your faith has saved you. Go in peace."*

CLOPAS: Just right then, a servant came running from Jairus' house. "Your daughter is dead," he gasped. "Don't bother the Rabbi anymore." Jairus turned to Jesus, devastation in his eyes. But when Jesus heard this, he replied loudly for all to hear . . .

MARY: [imitating Jesus] *"Don't be afraid. Only believe, and she will be made well."*

I was bewildered by Jesus's words, and I was not alone. It was the mix of their simplicity and the calm manner in which Jesus delivered them that compelled us. We didn't really have time to process how bizarre they were right then; we were all hooked and eager to follow Jesus and Jairus to Jairus' nearby home.

The sight of his wife and all their friends weeping outside did not affect Jairus. His anxieties had been replaced by a quietness that gave no evidence of emotion on his part. He let Jesus lead him and his crying wife inside, along with Peter, John, and James. Outside, the crowds joined the mourners in crying and mourning for the little girl.

Some cried . . .

CLOPAS: [imitating crowd] "If only Jesus had gone a little faster or if he had not stopped, then maybe he could have saved this girl, Jairus' pride and joy."

MARY: *The noise of all the grievers drew Jesus back out*

of the house. Their grief was heartfelt and contagious. *Jesus said to them. "Stop crying. for she is not dead but asleep."*

CLOPAS: I was among those who stood before the house, keeping others from entering it. It was an easy task. Everyone had read the writing on the wall. It was too late. The girl was dead. Though inside, the unimaginable was about to occur. Later, I was told that Jesus took the girl by the hand and called out,

MARY: *"Child. get up!"*

CLOPAS: I CAN IMAGINE THE AIR IN THE ROOM WAS ELECTRIFIED WITH ANTICIPATION. Right then, she took a deep breath, and got up at once. Everyone there must have exhaled, I'm sure they'd been holding their breath. Jesus gave orders that she be given something to eat.

MARY: *Her parents covered her with kisses and their tears of joy. When Jesus came out. they came out with him. Jesus had instructed them not to tell anyone of what had happened*[52].

CLOPAS: Her father spoke briefly that, "Yes, she had been asleep and was no longer dying." Jairus looked sheepishly grateful, though the blood was not quite flowing back into his face yet. I thought he and his family

---

[52] Luke 8:40-56

would surely become supporters of Jesus, but he was afraid of losing his position in the local synagogue, and later criticized Jesus for healing a woman on the Sabbath. Afterward, he was thoroughly shamed by Jesus for his hypocritical legalism, although Jesus did not directly mention how he had healed his daughter on the Sabbath[53].

MARY: *The bizarre statement by Jairus left everyone, including me, emotionally exhausted. How could we process all that we had just witnessed? No longer swarmed as the victorious David of yore, the crowd slipped away from Jesus to attend to their plans for the Sabbath as morning dawned in the eastern sky. Soon, we went away back to Mary Magdalene's place in Cana. Jesus was smiling but drained, he didn't tell us what happened until later that day. We were joined by Susanna who wanted to follow and support Jesus alongside Mary Magdalene, Joanna, and other women like myself[54].*

CLOPAS: When we arrived, Mary Magdalene and Jesus's mother had cooked breakfast. After we ate, Jesus told me he needed to speak to me. My spirit sank in dread. I had seen Mary Magdalene talk some with him and knew what it was going to be about. Jesus wrapped a scarf around his head that

---

[53] Luke 13: 10-17

[54] Luke 8:3

partially covered his face, making it hard for people to recognize him, and we went for a walk.

After Jesus told me what he knew about my telling of his story, my jeremiad against Judas, and my behavior with Mary. He said, "Clopas, I love your passion. I see your potential, especially at telling your story. And, we are family, even if we do not always get along. I know how hard the idea of being cast out of your family would be. I fear that misunderstandings by my mother and half-brothers may sever our ties, perhaps forever. . . .

"But when you put your own ideas forth as if they were my ideas that was a sin, even if it was just an unwitting mistake of an overeager Clopas. You bore false witness about me. What you said could've gotten people killed. And you did not honor me or my steward Mary Magadalene with your outburst against Judas."

I said, "I'm sorry. It won't happen again. But I don't really see what you are doing. It's hard to wrap my mind around it."

MARY: *Jesus replied, "So you're trying to make sense of my teachings and ministry. I would commend you Clopas, because you see, unlike many, that you do not see.*

It is when you forget this truth that you turn away from me, proclaiming your own passions instead of relying on me. It is then that you imagine yourself to be me and speak for me.

"And so I will help you find healing in this arena of your soul. I need you to practice your love for me and your love for us all, by taking care of yourself. This can be done. Mary Magdalene will pay for you to take care of Lazarus for Martha and Mary. And she will pay for Martha and Mary to help take care of you. I myself will send off my twelve apostles soon. During that time when they are on their own, I plan to rest in Bethany at the house of Mary, Martha, and Lazarus. I will be there to help you. I want you to get stronger, to learn to be mindful of others, to remove the weeds that threaten to corrupt your soul."

CLOPAS: He continued, "I also know of your feelings for Mary. She is a wonderful woman and someday she will make a good wife. But she too suffers in her own way. You must be mindful not to increase her suffering. You must honor her, as I honored her when her will clashed with mine."

I replied, "As you wish. But I am worried about Judas. I don't trust him."

MARY: [imitates Jesus] *"You leave Judas to me. My father knows well the hearts of all who are with me and shares with me what I need to know. Do not trust Judas, trust me!"*

CLOPAS: We embraced. It was lunchtime when we returned. There was a big meal waiting. Jesus sat with his mother.

I was going to sit with him, but Peter and John asked to speak with me aside first. I had barely met them then and didn't know what to expect.

They wanted to talk with me about how I had appointed myself to be a body-guard of Jesus. My eagerness to help Jesus blinded me to the fact that if someone had tried to kill Jesus, I would have been the easiest route to go through. Peter and John expressed that it was wrong to appoint myself guard. Peter pointed out that I had never even used the short swords that they kept for self-protection.

And they meant well, but I was easy to wound. I was sure that I could learn and certain that my willingness to lay down my life for Jesus would compensate for any other weaknesses. They made it clear that while Jesus was with them, the apostles, I was not to "protect" Jesus.

This rejection made it hard for me to enjoy the meal with them. I ate, but I had withdrawn into my inner world. I might as well have eaten off among the beggars on the street.

MARY: *Many times early on that was Clopas's way to*

react to conflicts.

After the meal together, Jesus spoke briefly with his mother in private. We could not hear them, but apparently she had wanted him to return home with her for his time of rest.

CLOPAS: But Jesus knew that the eyes of his brothers were darkened, just as she did not understand him. He wanted to sow seeds in us who were fertile fields waiting his tending.

MARY: *Jesus's mother stormed off. Shortly after, Mary Magdalene and Jesus spoke with me. I had told them how much I wanted to be among Jesus's supporters and to follow him. But they said I was not ready to be with them. I too had to heal. Jesus promised that he soon would come and help me to heal in Bethany. They also convinced me to let Clopas take care of Lazarus. They promised that they would work with Clopas. They would help him to accept my lack of romantic interest in him so that we could be part of the same community. I accepted. Because of Jesus, I let Clopas remain in my life.*

CLOPAS: It was another miracle. He continued to save us from our deep wounds, including the wounds we inflicted on each other.

MARY: *And, he continues to be the heart of us.*

CLOPAS: Isn't that the truth!

[Both laugh and shake their heads.]

Jesus and Us

MARY: *Mary Magdalene escorted Clopas and me on an uneventful return trip home. Clopas kept his distance from me, mostly interacting with Mary. When we arrived home, Judas was there, and I was so glad to see him. Mary had brought a message for Judas that Jesus wanted Judas to come to him. But Judas did not leave right away. Instead, we all ate together after our long trip.*

CLOPAS: I was quiet most of the time, helping Lazarus eat. My Mary talked about Jesus, the official, and the synagogue leader. I chimed in, recounting the moment when the woman touched Jesus, and then Mary continued with the rest of the story.

MARY: *Mary Magdalene explained the new arrangement in Lazarus's care to Martha, Lazarus, Judas, and me. She had to explain it more than once because it was unheard of that a person like Lazarus with no wealth would have a servant. This was a privilege normally reserved for the wealthy. It likewise was unheard of that anyone would get payed to help a misfit like Clopas. Judas showed some irritation but did not comment on it. Martha was glad for the money and the help. Lazarus clumsily embraced Clopas like a brother.*

CLOPAS: Lazarus and I began to become friends. He was often lonely. I liked the idea of taking care of him initially since he was Mary's brother,

but I was also afraid of it. It was
the creation of a new way of being, a
new routine. One that did not work at
first. Conflicts emerged between
everybody, not just Mary and me.
Although, our conflicts were probably
the worst.

MARY: *It felt overwhelming to care for Clopas, in
addition to Cazarus. For Clopas gave us more trouble
than help at first. And, we knew how to take care of
Cazarus, even though it was hard. We didn't know how
to take care of Clopas. He was so eager to be near me, it
drained my energy.*

*Most of the difficulties were in the details. For example,
Martha and I usually picked Cazarus up by his arms
and his legs to carry him to a place where he could
relieve himself. Now, whose place would Clopas take?
Martha was stronger than me, but she was also busier. I
didn't want to do work with Clopas, but to my chagrin, I
found myself doing so anyway. Clopas and I would move
Cazarus together, which was hard on Cazarus since we
were not that strong. Together, we dragged him on a rug
whenever he needed to relieve himself. One time we didn't
make it and Cazarus grew unusually upset as a wet stain
darkened his robes. Cikewise, Clopas was supposed to
bathe Cazarus, but initially he hardly knew how to bathe
himself.*

CLOPAS: Well, I did know how to bathe,
but bathing just complicated matters
for me. I had so many things on my
mind, and I didn't like to bathe. I

didn't bathe much as a blind beggar
and my experiences with it were bad.
This added to how my mind raced all
the time, and it was hard to slow down
and just take care of Lazarus or
myself.

MARY: *Neither Martha nor I really wanted to show
him how to help, so Lazarus tried but it was hard for him.
Lazarus was slowly losing more and more control over
his body as the illness that had begun by robbing him of
the ability to walk affected the rest of him. It made
Lazarus speak with a slur. His difficulty speaking made
him use short, clipped sentences most of the time. He had
trouble describing some of his needs to Clopas since he
was unused to having to do so. Martha and I always
knew what he needed, sometimes before Lazarus even
knew himself. When Clopas dressed or undressed
Lazarus, he often tangled Lazarus's arms in his robes.
Once Clopas let Lazarus's head fall back hard against
the ground. And, at first, everything took at least twice
as long as it should have.*

CLOPAS: Lazarus wanted to be friends
with me, but you can imagine that for
a man in his position, it was hard.
Lazarus's world was limited. It was a
glimpse of how much worse my life
could have been if I had been stuck at
home all the time and unable to beg.
Lazarus demanded much of my time, time
I also wanted to try to spend with
Mary. Although, it seemed like the
only thing I could do right by her was

to stay away, which I did for the most part.

MARY: *It's true: he did manage to keep out of my company except for mealtimes and when we worked with Lazarus together. And, Clopas was a different person at those times. He seemed more focused and somehow, happier.*

CLOPAS: Yes, that's right. I wasn't lost in thought or sad, as I normally was. But after every time I spoke with Mary, afterward I would remember every word we said and worry that I had said the wrong thing. It is sad how caught up I was in the world of words back then, when the real issues between us had little to do with words.

And Martha, I couldn't forgive Martha for how she tricked me into upsetting Mary. I wasn't thinking straight when I first met Mary. I was grasping for straws. Later, I felt guilty that my mistake had set us off on the wrong foot, and I blamed Martha for it. Martha was usually polite with me, but I didn't trust her, and so I wasn't always polite in return. I was moody, embarrassed by how hard it was to learn how to take care of both Lazarus and myself.

When it got bad for me, I'd go and sit out among the beggars again to get away from everyone. And, sometimes, I didn't tell them about it and I would lose track of time, as I got caught up in daydreams about Mary and my dreams of a life with her. I wish I'd been thinking about Jesus and his teachings, but what can I say? This woman had entranced me.

[The two exchange a loving glance.]

Soon, Mary Magdalene came to visit again. Almost immediately, I complained to her about Mary and Martha's lack of instruction in Lazarus's care. She was dismayed over the "care" given to me by Mary and Martha.

MARY: *No one was happy. Martha and I had assumed that we would receive Clopas's earnings, since we had the responsibility to provide for him. But Clopas seemed to think he needed his own money. This was payback from him for how we treated him. It also was folly. Mary Magdalene paid Martha and me too little. We needed Clopas's money too, but we struggled to get him to share it! Clopas was no manager of money. Like he said, he'd never cared about money, but* [she laughs] *he sure knew how to abuse it to get attention. This made even Lazarus upset with Clopas. And then, Mary Magdalene, who now distrusted us, kept dropping in to check on us, wanting an accounting of the funds she'd distributed. She also wanted a plan for what we were going to do with Clopas. She wanted a clearer division of duties between Martha and me, which led to more conflicts.*

I blamed Clopas for the mess. It was his unreasonableness with me that had upset our relations together and with Mary Magdalene. And so I got my revenge on Clopas for complaining to Mary Magdalene by also complaining to Mary that Clopas had repeatedly eyed me lasciviously and that his behavior toward me could be lewd.

CLOPA: I wasn't blameless, but I often just couldn't help staring at her. . . .

MARY: *Yes, and then I read a lot of my baggage into Clopas back then. . . .*

From there with Mary Magdalene, I also griped about the way Clopas complicated the decisions on how we spent his money. How he insisted on participating even in many mundane decisions as a way to force me to interact with him more.

CLOPAS: This upset Mary Magdalene. She asked me to keep my eyes to myself in regards to Mary and promised that my wages might be reduced if I continued to bother her. But that just heaped oil on the fire. I didn't care about the money. I felt so misunderstood. I wanted to start over again with Mary but that was not possible. So I was left wrestling my demons, which got in the way of everything else. And, Mary Magdalene was too caught up with arrangements for Jesus's women supporters to give my problems much time.

MARY: *And we all needed the money. Things began to get out of control, as we once ran out of oil for cooking and I had to dip into the alabaster vase I had anointed Jesus's feet from and that was to be my dowry. But then, finally, Jesus came to save us again.*

CLOPAS: The time with Jesus felt magical.

MARY: *He sensed right away why we had failed, knowing that in any community, there are the occasional bumps that develop bruises. All of our relationships with each other had suffered. My eyes were so focused inward, toward my own worries and problems that I never took the time to think of possible creative solutions to our communal dysfunctions. That took the master carpenter.*

CLOPAS: First off, Jesus dealt with Mary and me. He spoke with us separately and then together. He suggested that when Mary wanted me to back off that she step backwards as a sign to me. Jesus told me that if I truly cared about Mary then I would listen to her. He also privately counseled me, giving me practical advice on how to avoid mental adultery. He showed me that thinking of women in this way only poisoned my ability to relate to them and treat them with the honor they deserved as human beings, not simply objects.

MARY: *This cleared the air somewhat so that it was*

easier for Clopas and me to work together. Jesus also took my place in moving Lazarus with Clopas. He saw that this was a temporary solution and after a little thought he began to design what he called a moveable mat-seat. He needed some carpentry tools and supplies, which Mary Magdalene and Judas procured for him.

CLOPAS: Both Lazarus and I were fascinated by Jesus's carpentry skills and work as he created the moveable mat-seat. Lazarus seemed especially interested since it was for him. This gave us something new to talk about. Jesus made a wheel for the bottom up front and handles that protruded from the back. I found the design and construction of the seat to be interesting, but even more interesting was Jesus himself as a carpenter. It was like he was God's tool crafted to create other tools to help us. And when he finished, it took only one person to move Lazarus, although it still took two to load him onto the moveable mat-seat.

Jesus amazed me. Who would work during his time of rest? But the moderate amounts of carpentry work Jesus did seemed to give him growing amounts of energy. A certain truth became flesh for me as I watched him. For, unlike me, Jesus's words were not empty. His words, often simple and repetitive, came with action, and something real was created where there once was nothing. I spoke and claimed much but crafted no real change. But soon I would be transformed. . . .

When he finished the first moveable mat-seat, Jesus insisted that I take Lazarus outside and see how it worked there. The ride was too bumpy, and Lazarus fell off the mat-seat with a huff. So Jesus began work on a second mat-seat that could function outside and after two attempts it did. Then, in a surprising move, Jesus asked me to give Lazarus the necessary skills to make a successful beggar. Then, there would be more income for the household.

MARY: *The money Lazarus made helped him feel as though he were a contributing member of the household and not a drain. This eased some of his tension, along with our own. Jesus helped bring all our finances to a state of health. He persuaded Clopas to let earnings go into a common purse, which Jesus also contributed to during his month with us. Then I no longer had to draw from my dowry. But it also raised the matter of who would keep the common purse, Martha or I? I had more experience with the management of money than she did. But she was in charge of meal planning and preparation. And, since that was our biggest regular expense, I let Martha take charge. Martha put together a budget for expenses. Jesus and I created a plan for Clopas's assistance of Lazarus and our assistance of*

Clopas. This restored Mary Magdalene's trust in us and gave Clopas guidance in how to take care of Lazarus. It also gave him better things to do than to mope around with beggars on his own time.

CLOPAS: We all took long walks together that did not involve any conversation. Instead, Jesus insisted that we repeat to ourselves a truth we needed. For example, I would repeat something like, "Help me to see more, Lord."

MARY: I would pray, "Help me to forgive me."

CLOPAS: Things improved quickly because of Jesus's presence and guidance. But he couldn't do away with my attraction to Mary. Sensing this, Mary kept her distance, and it remained a thorn in my flesh. For to be around her animated me, as it still does. For awhile it was the only thing that brought me life. Sight, by itself, had been an unexpected source of many difficulties and new sorrows that I had been unable to see before. But slowly, I began to notice that I was also invigorated by being with Jesus or pondering his teachings, something I was encouraged to do regularly. And when I saw Jesus benefit from his carpentry work, it made me seek the same focus when I helped Lazarus. Soon, it was a pleasure to help Lazarus. I grew more capable and felt more confident in my abilities.

It didn't hurt that Jesus also helped me to get stronger. [Laughs] He *tried* to teach me carpentry. In addition to the moveable mat-seats, he made some furniture for Mary and Martha. I helped some, but not a lot. I was and always will be clumsy. I would sometimes wreck Jesus's work. He would tell me he had also made mistakes at first, forgave me, and insisted that I continue to learn.

Jesus felt that I was ready for an independent project, so he asked me to carve a walking stick for Lazarus. It kept me busy for weeks. He couldn't use it, but Lazarus loved it, even more than the moveable mat-seat. As for me, I was glad that carpentry distracted me from Judas's frequent visits.

MARY: *Like the other apostles, Judas had been sent by Jesus to travel from village to village, proclaiming the good news and healing[55]. However, he managed to get villages that were closer by, since he also had to remain in contact some with possible supporters. He came to visit Jesus and me. While Jesus worked with Clopas, we would sit together and talk. Judas knew how to engage me in respectful conversation, and he was sure not to gawk and pawn over my physical appearance. And his*

---

[55] Luke 9: 2-6.

voice! It was like honey, exactly the sort of voice you'd
expect from the rabbi who read aloud from the Torah at
the Synagogue.

[Clopas rolls his eyes]

Judas talked some about his time spent following Jesus
and his management of the common purse. Some of the
other followers were jealous of him. I could relate. Other
women had always been jealous of me because of my
beauty, even my own sister. Little did they know, I
considered my beauty a curse until Jesus redeemed me.

Now, I knew what I was doing when I mentioned the
dowry I'd saved for a husband. Did his head snap with
attention then! Judas was no longer in favor with his
father and had little money of his own. The dowry I
could provide was uncommon. As with Nathanael's
wedding, the groom's family usually provided a dowry
for the family of the bride. But . . . my situation was
unique. . . . And, just as I'd hoped, Judas began to court
me.

CLOPAS: Oy vey! Judas found excuses to
come visit often. Once, while he
visited, I asked Jesus if he would
teach me how to use the small swords
they carried with them for self-
defense. He had already taught me how
to use one to sharpen the other. But
he would not teach me how to use it so
I could be one of his guards again.
After Jesus left, Judas told me he
would teach me how to use a sword.
Sword fighting was a part of Judas's

broad education. It was the first time he had ever done anything for me, and I was pleased, but still a bit cautious.

Judas grabbed two pieces of wood and tossed me one. Before I could even get my grip on it, he knocked it out of my hands. He laughed, picked it up, and proceeded to show me how to hold it with my right hand. Our lesson continued painfully, as he made it clear that I would never match his skill.

But this fuelled my desire to learn. And he also gained power over me, since he had knowledge and skill I too wanted to possess. I could no longer avoid him during his visits.

MARY: *In another one of Judas's visits, Jesus explained that he liked to craft his stories in part from his own life experience. Apparently, Judas had inspired Jesus when he left his family of origin and began to follow after him. Eventually the words he used became a part of the parable of the prodigal son. This embarrassed Judas. He was not used to being called a prodigal.*

Jesus had also been inspired by his mother. Not long after Joseph died, money was tight. She had been given ten silver coins. She thought she needed them all to provide for her seven children. When she lost a coin, she was determined to find it. Lighting a candle, she swept the house, and she asked Jesus to help her search carefully until she found it. When she found it, she was so happy that she decided to throw a party to celebrate[56].

CLOPAS: The story seemed absurd at first, but then it dawned on me that Jesus's mother had found joy in looking for the coin. It was the same type of purposeful activity that Jesus found joy in when he worked as a carpenter. The value of the lost coin was not of this world. It was personal; it came from within, from God. It was like how the power of God came from within Jesus to save him from starvation as a child. And, since it comes from God, often through absorption in purposeful activity, it had no necessary connection to what this world says value is.

I began to think of my romantic attraction to Mary in a similar way. It was absurd. Why would this beautiful woman ever look my way? My chances of success were extremely low. But it was a desire I could not shake, and I trusted that God would not put it in me unless there was a purpose for it. It may have been twisted by my attempts to become more lovable, but I believed in my heart that the initial spark of attraction was not born of

---

[56] **Luke 15:8-9**

me. I felt that I could see her spirit shine, and I knew that this inner knowing came from something greater than me. It kept me at Mary and Martha's house when I could have become a beggar again, this time pretending to be blind, and lived my life the way I wanted. I had heard of some who used their considerable verbal talents, like my own, to make enough money to live comfortably for a beggar.

You'd think that it would have been easy. After all, Jesus gave me sight, and I was able to develop a relationship with him. Wouldn't this have been enough to bind me to Jesus for life? But I still failed, and I still needed to change so many of my thoughts and habits. I suppose it was easier to focus on my feelings for Mary and allow the deeper work of Jesus to change me over time.

MARY: *God works in mysterious ways. Clopas was an irritant for me in some ways bad and in others, good. He made me uncomfortable, yes, but the force of his attraction also told me that there might be something missing between Judas and I. You see, Clopas reminded me of my own love for Jesus when I first encountered him. Passion, adoration, and an undying loyalty – I knew Clopas felt these for me, but I could not see any of those from Judas. A small voice in the back of my head told me that this mattered. It reminded me of the words my mother told me in the dawn of my womanhood when I hoped not to stir up or awaken love until the appropriate time*[57]. *Unsure, I stalled when Judas's interest in marriage became obvious.*

It seems obvious now that Judas was not a man of integrity. I had an inkling of this that spread across my heart as Judas grew distant with time. But with Judas's distance came some of my old doubts and insecurities. Jesus had entered my life, made a new life possible, but he didn't get rid of all of the old voices. They remained to torment me. Was I truly worthy of love and acceptance?

Jesus knew I struggled. He knew how much I hated my past, how I could not erase the shame and guilt. Because he knew I could read, Jesus helped me to write a letter to my past self. I told my old self that I forgave her and that she'd been the victim of hard times. I told her to let go of all the blame she carried. It was not her fault that her god-father was so ungodly. I told her that I loved her no matter what she had done. I asked her to start practicing forgiveness, especially for the men who had taken advantage of her. I promised her that someday she would meet a man who would respect her. Who would honor her and her desire to be honored as a married woman is honored. She would meet a man who she could trust, who would never treat her as a possession or an object to gratify his sexual desires. And if she didn't ever marry, she would still live a fulfilling life because she had Jesus.

---

[57] **Song of Solomon 2:7**

It was a hard letter to write together. After we worked on it, I kept it and would read it whenever the old voices got strong. Jesus helped me grieve my past, and in this way, I began to find healing.

Mary's Frustration with Clopas and Clopas's Frustration with Mary

MARY: *Jesus's help spilled over into other parts of my life. It helped me to learn to vent my frustrations with Clopas instead of bottling them up to fester within me. I couldn't write them down, but there were so many times I was frustrated with him that I still remember what it was like.*

CLOPAS: Thankfully, she didn't share this with me back then or we wouldn't be here today. It's like one of those psalms where the writer vents to God and God just takes it. We share them to show how radically Jesus had to transform us to make us possible.

MARY: *Yes Clopas, you know I love you. One of things I love about you is that you've humbled yourself to accept that this is how I felt about you.*

[pause, Clopas sits down while Mary steps forward and looks upwards.]

"I cannot stand him. He wants what is not his. He's so strange, so needy, so full of himself. He just knows that I'm 'going to be his'. It unnerves me. I wish he would accept me, just as I had to accept that Jesus did not want me as his wife. I may have been a prostitute, but that doesn't make me desperate, ready to step into the arms of any man interested in marrying me.

"And he's helpless. He may have gotten away with letting others do everything 'unimportant' for him before when he was blind, but not anymore. I mean, I'm glad to

be among those who help him, but I don't want to be his keeper. I have dreams. They do not include becoming the wife of a court jester-pretender. My worse nightmare is to be enslaved to take care of someone who, not unlike Lazarus, can hardly take care of himself for the rest of my life. Where is the joy in that?

"And then there's his politics. Clopas takes such strong positions on so many things. He's no longer a harmless blind beggar. People who speak like him get killed. And I don't want to be a widow, nor the wife of man more in love with his ideas than he is with me.

"He's not like Jesus at all. Jesus is present with the people around him. He does not revere the state, but he also knows his calling. He's like a fountain of blessings for others. Clopas is a fire show. He's putting on a show to get me to turn a blind eye to how he is a short, underdeveloped, former beggar, who often still seems blind.

"And, I am not going to take whatever crumb falls off the master's table. It's crazy but Jesus makes me feel like I deserve to be happy, secure and in love with all my heart, mind, strength, and soul. Clopas is not what I deserve. He can't even engage in a regular conversation with people. He wants to be the star of the show. It's too much.

"Please God help him to fall out of love with me and to move on. I want the best for him, but I know that's not me. I would resent him for the rest of my life if we were bound together. I don't want that; I want to be happy.

"And, what about Judas? He's exceptional! He's polite,

understanding, connected, knowledgeable about the Torah, and has even traveled to Rome. He's the best spoken man I have ever met and he seems to like me! He may not like me as much as he did at first, but that's normal. That happens with everyone. The new wine of love gets replaced with duty and warm feelings. Although, I cannot feel much warmth in his eyes. I mean if there's anything I can say about Clopas is that he is sincere. His eyes are not as intense, and I can see that he does care about me. His attention is not the same kind of attention that my former clients bestowed upon me. I'm sad Clopas cannot seem to woo my heart. I don't know. . . .

"I don't want to be caught like this between a good, weak man and a strong, handsome, successful but . . . not-so-good man. Oy vey! It drives me crazy. I wanted to put that burning anxiety behind me, but it keeps returning. What calms my mind is to remember Jesus's words, [Mary steps back and kneels at the feet of Clopas, looking into his eyes.] *"*

CLOPAS: Mary, let Clopas be. Accept that he shall remain a thorn for you for a while, just as Judas shall remain a mystery for you for a while. Do not try to fix or to solve either, instead, just remember your time at my feet, and let your tears continue to flow as you continue to heal." [Mary weeps and Clopas raises her to sit next to him for a spell.]

CLOPAS: [Standing and stepping forward] It

brings tears to my eyes to remember the hurt that Mary went through back then. Like I said, it's like those psalms that express not only praise, but also lament to God.

MARY: [Standing up again and facing upward as Clopas steps back] *Lord, why do you reject me? Why do you hide your face from me?*

CLOPAS: [They alternate who stands up and faces God. Outstretching hands.] From my youth, I have been afflicted and near death.

MARY: [again stands up and clasps hands together upwards] *I suffer Your horrors; I am desperate*[58]. [Hangs her head low for a spell, until Clopas comes behind her and puts his arms around her. They briefly kiss and she returns to her seat, while he remains before the audience.]

CLOPAS: Was *God* responsible for *their* suffering? No, but God is big and strong enough to accept our hurts and anger. I understand this. And I praise God that Jesus helped her learn how to express and then let go of her emotions, because I too was mired in my own frustrations back then. They sounded something like this. . . . [Similarly, faces upwards]

"I am not an apostle. I am not going

---

[58] **Psalm 88:14-5.**

to be among Jesus's twelve chosen ones. And, I don't know what Jesus means by the word apostle. If you are one, I think you are supposed to spread the good news of Jesus to the world. Maybe, I can do that but I'm not Peter, a person who can easily spring into action. I hate to think about all the things I struggle with. It's only with God's strength and a small miracle that I'm here at all. I'm waiting for another miracle, like Mary giving me a chance. . . .

"I swear I could do it. I'd easily become worthy of her with a little encouragement from her. All it would take is faith 'the size of a mustard seed'. . . .

But that is not true; that's me twisting the words of Jesus again for my own purposes. I don't want to do that, but I do pray to the Father in heaven that she could see me differently. I'm no longer the mess I was when I first met her.

"Maybe Jesus is right. I need to love myself before I can love my neighbors, including Mary. That, along with my story of how I was saved by Jesus, could be my witness to the world. I do not need to blossom into Mary's betrothed. Maybe that's not what I am meant to become.

"But I sure wish it were. I no longer wish to see myself as an ex-beggar who cannot take care of himself, [stretches out his hands] hating my weak, clumsy hands. I despise my dreams of Mary, knowing that she won't even consider me. I wish to be Judas. I wish I were handsome and charismatic. [Hangs head and then looks upwards hands out-stretched] I don't know what to do. . . ."

[silence as Clopas holds this position for a moment and then shifts back into narrator mode]

Clopas's Enlightenment and Mary's Engagement to Judas[59]

CLOPAS: Months later, after much travel, Jesus gave his apostles a break to go visit their loved ones. For Jesus and Judas, they came to visit us in Bethany. When they arrived, Jesus was warmly welcomed by Martha as Judas was warmly welcomed by Mary. I stayed back to greet Jesus after Judas had left, as he usually did to attend to some business of God knows what.

MARY: *Soon it felt like old times. Both Martha and I fell into our habits of relating to Jesus. When I had heard that Jesus was coming, I did my share of tasks in advance so I could, like others rescued by Jesus[60], sit at his feet and listen to what he said[61]. Martha, however, wanted to outdo herself in the preparation of a meal, which kept her away from Jesus. Clopas, first took care of Lazarus who needed to rest so he could enjoy his time with Jesus later. And to stay busy, Clopas also helped Martha.*

Meanwhile, I asked Jesus to explain his message again. He called it his word and told me how he had recently sent out seventy paired disciples to every town and place

---

[59] based on Luke 10:38-42

[60] Luke 8:35

[61] Luke 10:39

where he himself was about to go[62]. *This gave him a little time to rest and to visit his mother and us. When he visited his mother he found her unhappy with him; some of Jesus's half-brothers had left on a path that might take them away for good. Jesus grimaced* [Mary grimaces] *and went back to his new family.*

CLOPAS: I drew near to listen. [imitates Jesus] "These disciples of mine," [sighs] "they started to argue about who'd be the greatest of them. In other words, who'd replace me as the head Rabbi if I were gone." Jesus sighed again. When they asked him to settle the matter he had taken a little child and had him stand next to him. [imitates Jesus] "Whoever receives this little child in my name receives me. And whoever receives me receives him who sent me. For whoever is least among you--this one is great."

MARY: *By this time, Martha had begun to cast worried eyes in Jesus's direction. There was plenty of time until dinner, but she had taken on too much. And, she did not have any real help, since Clopas had wandered off, drawn to Jesus's words as I had been.* [both smile] *So out of frustration, she came up and asked,* [imitates Martha] *"Lord, don't you care that my sister has left me to serve alone? So tell her to help me." Jesus looked up and answered her,*

---

[62] Luke 10:1

CLOPAS: [imitates Jesus] "Martha, Martha, you are worried and upset about many things, but one thing is necessary. Mary has made the right choice, and it will not be taken away from her.[63]"

MARY: *It's ironic when life repeats itself. Martha had wanted Jesus to declare her the greatest. Yet he instead embraced my decision to abide like a child at his feet. Martha declined to join us.*

CLOPAS: I pondered the meaning of Jesus's words for me. I thought to myself, "one thing is necessary? What was my choice? Do I remain in a state of unreality by fantasizing about marrying Mary, or do I simply follow Jesus? I had no claim to her, there had never been an 'us'. We just got saved by him at about the same time and owed him the world. Otherwise, what did we have in common?

I'd spent my life dreaming about a future that elevated myself but I didn't really think about who else would be there. I'd just wanted to get there so it wouldn't matter that I was so clumsy and different. Then, I'd somehow win someone who would love me for the best of me . . . whatever that was. . . .

So what is my decision? To let her go

---

[63] Luke 10: 40-42

and to remember my time at the feet of Jesus, to remember the stories he told, my own story, and the ways I remain blind. Ways that now have broken things between Mary and me for good. I can decide to open my eyes and see many of the ideas in my mind as dead branches that had born no fruit. And dead branches need to be pruned."

Then it slapped me square in the jaw. I was a slave to the idea that I could compete with Judas. I was chained to believe Mary would someday begin to view me differently. The realization was so overwhelming that I fled the room, finding a quieter room to weep. Self-pruning hurts. And, I knew it would continue to be hard.

MARY: *Soon after he had rebuked Martha, Jesus began another story about a Samaritan village that rejected him because he determined to journey to Jerusalem[64]. It was the same village where he'd helped a Samaritan woman and thought he had gained many followers[65]. But now she wanted him to be her husband, just as they wanted him to be their king. His eyes drifted to Martha who still wanted Jesus to be her husband. Jesus understood why she was trying to outdo herself as a host. It made him grimace again: so many wanted to claim him. They might've meant well but their desires would*

---

[64] Luke 9:53

[65] John 4:1-42

*have kept him from what waited in Jerusalem. He then
began to tell some short stories about the people who
wanted to join him along the way. He was on his last one
when Judas arrived.*

CLOPAS: [imitates Jesus] "Another also said,
'I will follow you, Lord, but first
let me go and say good-bye to those at
my house.' But I said to him, 'No one
who puts his hand to the plow and
looks back is fit for the kingdom of
God.[66]"

MARY: *This time Jesus's eyes drifted toward Judas, and
his face settled into another grimace. But then he rose to
greet Judas who had changed his clothing to more
splendid garb. Jesus remarked that he was the best
dressed of all of his disciples. Judas grinned. I don't
think he understood that it was not necessarily a
compliment. Jesus knew then that Judas had stopped
following him. Why he kept him around was a mystery,
but I certainly did not know the truth about Judas at the
time.*

*I excused myself to help Clopas load Lazarus onto the
moveable mat-seat. We would often do this together,
since it was not safe for one person to lift Lazarus by
himself. I found Clopas in the next room, rubbing his eyes
with the back of his arm. He looked at me and said,*

CLOPAS: I also think you made the right
choice, to abide with Jesus as the one
thing necessary. . . .

---

[66] Luke 9: 61-62

MARY: *Then he turned away, bent on his duty to Cazarus. This surprised me, and I managed to murmur my gratitude before I refocused on loading Cazarus onto his mat-seat. I quickly left, uncomfortable with the awkwardness and confused by the tumult of emotions rising within me. . . .*

Judas, Jesus, and I were soon joined by Cazarus who was wheeled over by Clopas. Cazarus looked tired but happy. Martha called us to dinner. It was a feast, she'd killed a lamb and made the meal that she knew Jesus liked the best. And it probably was the best meal that Martha had ever made. But it must have tasted like bitter herbs for her after Judas began the meal with a toast that ended with a request to Cazarus for my hand in marriage. Our rivalry, especially when it came to marriage, remained a rift between us and Judas's proposal had widened it considerably.

CLOPAS: Martha, Jesus, and I were struck by the proposal. Martha and I looked from Judas to Mary and then Lazarus. I then saw Jesus out of the corner of my eye. He bit his lip and looked at Lazarus. Lazarus said, "Let's let Mary decide."

MARY: *When Judas proposed my mouth fell open in surprise. Then Cazarus had given me the freedom of my choice, and I was doubly surprised. But when my gaze drifted back to Judas, I couldn't see anyone else. It was the sort of moment I had dreamed about. I said, "Yes, I will marry you, Judas. I love you." I hardly noticed when Martha steamed off and Clopas left the room. I definitely didn't notice Jesus's reaction. I can imagine he knew what was going on, but like Lazarus let me decide. No, right then it was just Judas and I, nothing else mattered.*

CLOPAS: I stepped outside the house and walked a short way down the road. My thoughts were, "It was real. Mary would marry Judas. Why, God? Why give me sight and then let me fall so hard for the wrong woman? Why can't I move on? Marriages are arranged. They are based on how one can provide. What could I provide Mary's family, besides more lessons for Lazarus on how to beg? God, I wish I was still blind."

Then Jesus came and found me. He embraced me and told me he loved me. I told him I had thought about the one thing necessary. I was going to stay and take care of Lazarus and myself. He said I would spring forth with living water because of the choice that I had made. Then he helped me dry my eyes so we could rejoin the celebration. For he and Judas would leave the next morning. And it was clear that Judas was happy, but Mary was ecstatic.

MARY: *I thought, "Judas wants me to be his wife! Thank you God. I knew you would provide."*

Lazarus's Death and A Crisis of Faith

CLOPAS: Soon Judas and Mary had an engagement ceremony where they signed a contract to be married. I did not attend.

MARY: I made sure it specified that provisions would be made for Lazarus and Martha so long as she was not married. I thought this would smooth over things between us, since this would encourage Judas to help find her a husband. But our rivalry it seems went too deep.

CLOPAS: Months passed. Mary, at first, remained elated over her engagement to Judas. Martha stewed. I became the intermediary between them. Lazarus lost more control of his body, including his ability to speak coherently. Judas and Mary were gone with Jesus most of the time. Mary went with him in part to get away from Martha, not me.

MARY: My time with Jesus and Judas was eye-opening in more ways than one. I traveled with the female supporters of Jesus, led by Mary Magdalene. During that time, I saw and learned a lot from Jesus, but I also learned a lot about Judas. He bought me gifts like white raisins and trinkets, for like I said, Judas was not good at the simple life. But he shared with me that he was saving up for something big. He wanted to buy land south of Jerusalem on which to build a synagogue. The synagogue would also be for Jesus and the others, but he had not told them about it. He figured they all were too idealistic, especially Jesus with his reluctance to establish a chain of command. So someone had to make it happen, for our current situation could not continue forever.

Later, he took me to a potter's field that he could acquire for thirty pieces of silver. He was going to use my dowry combined with his own savings, and other money he had procured, (which he said was from his mother) as collateral for a loan to build a synagogue. It was a good location, surely worth more than 30 pieces of silver. Judas probably was getting a good deal from someone for it, possibly with the help of his father.

This woke me up. I had been attracted to the Judas who had fled the evil ways of his father to follow Jesus. I became sorrowful, as my future no longer seemed secure. Judas had too much spare money for a follower of Jesus. This made him a thief, for where else would he get the money besides the common purse that he managed? But far worse was his plan to start his own synagogue. Such a move would sow divisions amongst Jesus and the others. If I married him, I would be "on his side," but apart from Jesus. I couldn't imagine a worse fate, but because of my marriage contract, I could not end the engagement without Judas's permission. And so I was trapped. The only one left for me was Cazarus. . . .

CLOPAS: But then, one winter morning, I found Lazarus very weak. Mary and Martha came and saw their brother was dying. We all thought of Jesus. We knew from Judas that he was across the Jordan. I was sent to get him and to bring him back as soon as possible!

MARY: *Things between Martha and I had been full of conflict and negativity for some time, but when Lazarus started on the road toward death, it brought us back together. We both fasted and prayed for his life. We all prayed he would remain with us. But Lazarus, as best as I could understand him, prayed, "God's will be done...."*

CLOPAS: I was used to making local trips on my own, praying walks like the ones Jesus took us on together. But this felt more like when I was scrambling to get to the pool of Siloam. I was constantly on unfamiliar ground but I had taken Lazarus' walking stick with me. The stick and my own brand of personal intensity kept me going. I had honored my promise to Jesus to focus on the care of Lazarus, to be like Jesus for Lazarus. I repeated under my breath, "Jesus, save him," again and again as I doggedly searched day and night to find Jesus. For what difference does it make to a former blind man whether he could see or not? I knew what general direction to go in, completely trusted all my senses and the stick and asked for directions. I learned Jesus had gone across the Jordan to the place that John the Baptist had been baptizing earlier. Lots of people had been visiting him there. He remained there because of them so they would believe[67]. Finally, I found him and gasped, "Lord, the one you love is sick."

MARY: [imitates Jesus] *"This sickness will not end in death, but is for the glory of God, so that the Son of God can be glorified through it.[68]"*

CLOPAS: I fainted.

The moment I awoke, I asked his apostles, "Has he left?" I was told he had not. I begged their pardon. I had run day and night to get to Jesus in time for him to save Lazarus. "Why?" They did not know. It was two days later at their camp. Jesus had provided his own sleeping quarters for me while he went out to pray. "But he loves Lazarus. Why would he not go save him?"

I thought of the hard life of Lazarus and how important it had become for me to take care of him. I thought of Mary and Martha, how difficult their relationship had become and how Lazarus held them together. I remembered Jesus's words, "This sickness will not end in death. . . ." It didn't make sense. I demanded, "Where is he?" And then I felt my hunger and weakness, and Jesus

---

[67] John 10:40-42.

[68] John 11:3-4

returned.

MARY: [imitates Jesus] *"Clopas, you are indeed changing, for the better. There are few who would risk their life and health like you did for Lazarus. My disciples, let's go to Judea again.*[69]*"*

CLOPAS: They were astonished. [imitates disciples] "Rabbi, just now the Jews tried to stone you, and you're going there again?"

MARY: [imitates Jesus] *"Aren't there twelve hours in a day?"*

CLOPAS: We didn't understand so Jesus answered,

MARY: *"If anyone walks during the day, he doesn't stumble, because he sees the light of this world. If anyone walks during the night, he does stumble, because the light is not in him. Just ask our friend, Clopas, right?*[70]*"*

CLOPAS: We laughed, but it was odd. Why didn't he just wish Lazarus to be healed? Was he really going to bring Lazarus back from the dead? What he said next told me he would.

MARY: [imitates Jesus] *"Our friend Lazarus has fallen asleep, but I'm on my way to wake him up.*[71]*"*

CLOPAS: It seemed as if they were looking for excuses not to go back to

[69] John 11:5-7

[70] John 11:8-10

[71] John 11:11

Judea, because then they said, "Lord, if he has fallen asleep, he will get well." I looked at Jesus and saw he was calm. He looked at me as he said,

MARY: [imitates Jesus] *"Lazarus has died. I'm glad for you that I wasn't there so that you may believe. But let's go to him.*[72]*"*

CLOPAS: And I thought, "Believe what? That you can just toy with the anxieties of us normal folks about death?" I was not the only non-believer. Thomas, nicknamed "The Twin" because of his physical similarities to Jesus in appearance, was also a pessimist. He had long expected to die for Jesus, so it came as no surprise when said,

MARY: *"Let's go so that we may die with him*[73]*."*

CLOPAS: And so we all left.

It was a quiet journey, maybe like the one Abraham made with Isaac. Jesus seemed irritated. He must have expected that we would have caught on. I remembered the daughter of the synagogue leader, but my insides churned at the thought of the death of Lazarus. I had denied the shock of his illness throughout my trek to get to Jesus. Now, my weariness made me

---

[72] John 11: 12, 14-15

[73] John 11:15

embrace Lazarus's mortality and my own. Jesus had let him die, like he might let me die. I had to stop wishing Lazarus would be brought back to life. Would Jesus really save him? There was nothing more to do now but keep following Jesus. I had no choice.

My thoughts, as they so often did, turned to Mary. She told me to tell Jesus that the one he loved was sick. I had not failed her. What if she blamed me for Lazarus's death? I did everything I could for her and him. I hoped she could see that it wasn't my fault. But it didn't matter. I wouldn't be with her anymore, and that was probably all the better. I still adored her. I still wanted to feast my eyes upon her. I still wanted to hear her laugh. I still remembered her crying over Jesus's feet. I still remembered the look on her face when Jesus raised her up, and she stood strong, full of faith and love. My God, I had wanted to earn a look like that from her.

Maybe if I'd gotten Jesus back in time, she would've turned away from marrying Judas. Oddly enough, Judas didn't show any emotion over the death of his future bride's brother. He lagged behind us. I couldn't and didn't want to read him. Everytime I saw him, I was reminded of my failings.

It took us four days to go through what I had done in a day and a half. I actually felt like I was one of the disciples. There was a respect from others as we traversed the rough terrain. I'd developed calluses where there was once only weakness.

When we arrived in Bethany, it turned out that Lazarus had been in the tomb for four days, beyond the pale of hope for a resurrection of his spirit. Many professional mourners had come to comfort Martha and Mary. As soon as Martha heard that Jesus was coming, she came out to meet him.

MARY: *I stayed seated in our house[74]. I had felt similarly as Clopas felt. I remembered the miracle Jesus performed in Cana but this was my brother who I had taken care of a great deal for his entire life. There was no reason for him to die and rot in a tomb.*

I had never felt closer to my sister than for the four days that we prayed together for Lazarus. We were united as one family. There was no more rivalry between us. We just prayed for Lazarus and waited for Jesus. But Jesus did not come, and I was there when Lazarus drew his last breath.

Then, I did not weep for him, because I thought Jesus

---

[74] John 11:20

could still bring him back. He'd only been dead for a little while, so his spirit could still be restored. I paid for him to be wrapped in linen clothing and put in a tomb to keep his body ready for when Jesus arrived. And still no Jesus. Instead, my heart sank deeper and deeper into doubt. Did Clopas fail me? Why was Jesus not here? Why let us go through this? I put aside these thoughts and tried to pray some more. Martha and I drifted apart as the mourners came and did their best to share the grief burden with us. Finally, Jesus arrived.

CLOPAS: Martha said,

MARY: *"Lord, if you had been here, my brother wouldn't have died. Yet even now I know that whatever you ask from God, God will give you."*

CLOPAS: "Your brother will rise again," Jesus told her. Martha, without missing a heartbeat said,

MARY: *"I know that he will rise again in the resurrection at the last day.[75]"*

CLOPAS: It was what Jesus had taught us. It was her turn to shine, for Mary was overwhelmed.

Jesus looked her in the eye and said, "I am the resurrection and the life. The one who believes in me, even if he dies, will live. Everyone who lives and believes in me will never

---

[75] John 11:21-24

die . . . ever. Do you believe this?[76]"

Martha did not flinch. There was no hesitation, no moment of fear and trembling over Jesus's words. I thought, "To never die? That's absurd! Surely, the spirit of the people of Israel will continue forever, but I never was comfortable with talk about the next life. I thought of it as an empty pursuit by people who didn't want to take responsibility for this life. Or maybe I just didn't want to think about death at all. That was probably more of it. . . ."

Martha replied,

MARY: *"Yes, Lord, I believe you are the Messiah, the Son of God, who comes into the world.[77]"*

CLOPAS: The words of belief were all there, but as she went back, I'd swear that Jesus shed a tear. The truth is our emotions were so heavy, we were all bawling, waiting for Jesus to lead us on. Some were looking around, fearful of the others who were there and how they might slip off to get the authorities to come for us all.

MARY: *When Martha came in, she called for me. We withdrew into her room. When she told me, "The rabbi is*

---

[76] John 11: 25-26

[77] John 11: 27

here . . . and is calling for you.[78]" she stuck the pin in where it would hurt the most. I assumed I had let Jesus down. Perhaps, it was something I did or didn't do that made him not come sooner? I didn't dwell on it. I got right up and went straight to Jesus, not seeing anyone. Apparently, everyone followed me. I fell at his feet crying, "Lord, if you . . . had been here . . . my brother . . . would not have died![79]" The only thing to do was to cry. I saw Clopas behind Jesus crying. Judas was nowhere in sight.

CLOPAS: This was the same Mary I had fallen in love with. This time I did not stare. I could only weep. All of our efforts, all of our prayers, all of my anxiety to get to Jesus dissolved into a huge wave of tears. It swept any pretense of belief out from under me. I was there with Mary weeping. Others were there too, but we had been with Lazarus and Jesus so much and now, we had both lost our way.

Jesus felt this. From deep within him came what felt like a lightning flash that radiated righteous anger and drew us to him. It felt like he was ready to grab the horns of the one responsible for so much rebellion and slay him. He asked quietly, "where

---

[78] John 11:28

[79] John 11:29, 32

have you put him?"

"Lord, come and see," many said.

MARY AND CLOPAS: ***Jesus wept[80].***

CLOPAS: And the waves of grief over death's grip fell all around us. The waves were not stilled, or were they? I was so soaked that I could not tell.

MARY: *I likewise cannot remember much about this time of sorrow. Some said,*

CLOPAS: "see how he loved him!"

MARY: *But others, seeing Clopas, said,*

CLOPAS: "Couldn't he who opened the blind man's eyes also have kept this man from dying?[81]"

MARY: *At that point, my eyes met Clopas's eyes, and I really saw him, as if for the first time. He was a mirror of me. I saw he loved Lazarus as if he were his own flesh and blood, and had done all he could to keep him from dying. I then sought Jesus's eyes, but he had let Lazarus die. And somehow, the love in their eyes appeared the same to me. I stopped weeping. Jesus no longer wept. Instead, he had the intense expression on his face that was there when he said,*

CLOPAS: "Let the one without sin cast the first stone."

MARY: *Or when he told Simon Iscariot that he. . . .*

---

[80] John 11:33-35

[81] John 11:36-37

CLOPAS: "had something to say to him."

MARY: *Or when he rebuked Martha with:*

CLOPAS: "it will not be taken away from her."

MARY: *But his face was even more focused, as if he were shoring up all his strength. He came to the tomb and said,*

CLOPAS: "Remove the stone."

MARY: *Martha, without thinking, spoke her truth. "Cord, he's already decaying. It's been four days."*

CLOPAS: [imitates Jesus] "Didn't I tell you that if you believed you would see the glory of God?[82]"

MARY: *At this, Martha withdrew from us. Jesus had pierced her heart. He had been a rabbi for her, and perhaps even a great husband if she kept at it. But that would never happen now.* CLOPAS: Martha had grown attached to Jesus, just as I was to Mary.

MARY: *Yes, I don't like to talk about my marriage with Clopas much when I share about Jesus. I don't want anyone to think that if they also become a follower of Jesus that they'd be blessed with a wonderful husband or wife. Jesus never promised that to us.*

[Clopas squeezes Mary's hand]

CLOPAS: Then, shortly after Jesus said:

---

[82] John 11:38-40

MARY: *"Remove the stone!"*

CLOPAS: He raised his eyes and said,

MARY: *"Father, I thank you that you heard me. I know that you always hear me, but because of the crowd standing here I said this, so they may believe you sent me."*

CLOPAS: And then, Jesus shouted as loud as I have ever heard anyone ever shout before, "LAZARUS, COME OUT![83]" And Lazarus walked out. He was a mummy, bound hand and foot with linen strips, his face wrapped in a cloth. He mumbled something, but we couldn't hear him. So Jesus told us to,

MARY: *"loose him and let him go.[84]"*

CLOPAS: Now, I've never swum underwater. But seeing Lazarus coming back to life reminded me of my own miracle, that moment when I lifted my head out of the water, air began to flow back into me and the mud fell from my eyes. I saw myself for the first time ever. As I saw Lazarus breathing and walking again and his face freed from the linens, I realized I'd not only gained my sight but been released from the curse of death as well. Once Mary had momentarily let go of her brother, I stepped in to grip

---

[83] John 11:41-43

[84] John 11:44

Lazarus in a hug. Then, I handed him his walking stick.

MARY: *Jesus had loved Lazarus, Clopas, Martha, and me, but our faith needed to be put to the test. And even if I failed to believe in Jesus before, I was still with Jesus and Lazarus and Clopas. I didn't see Martha, and I didn't care. What I did see were many faces gazing upon Jesus as I had first gazed upon him.*

And, right then, I did what felt right. I hugged Clopas. You should have seen his face. It took him completely by surprise. He had the most surprised, pleased expression on his face. I think Judas saw me hug Clopas, but I couldn't be sure, because when I glanced up again, Judas had disappeared.

CLOPAS: Later, we would find out that he had gone to his father to tell him what Jesus had done[85]. The "prodigal" son returned home. But right then and there, there was too much elation over the rebirth of Lazarus to let any sad thoughts come to us. And, I was elated for two reasons. For if Lazarus could be raised from the dead then surely Mary could fall in love with a former blind beggar who'd been transformed into a disciple of Jesus!

---

[85] John 11:46

On the Way with Jesus

MARY: *From that point on, we began to form a new us, as we were changed by Jesus. It was hard not to be joyful with the new Lazarus.*

CLOPAS: We helped Lazarus together and enjoyed every minute we spent together. It wasn't a lot of time, but it was enough. Enough to make a new reality for us become possible as we drew to the end of our time with Jesus.

MARY: *Judas and Martha grew more distant, literally for him and figuratively for her, as she seemed to withdraw into her own world in the wake of Jesus's rebuke of her. Jesus had left for Galilee and Judas went with him. Judas knew I was aware he took from the common purse. I was also aware that a good tree does not bear bad fruit. Also, in my heart, I could not say I'd want to marry Judas without his air of "security,"* [Clopas laughs] *and so I knew I did not love him. I could not marry him and follow Jesus. So I waited for Judas to come to end our engagement. But instead John came with a request from Jesus for Clopas and me to join him in Galilee before he came to Jerusalem for the Passover.*

CLOPAS: The three of us made the journey in two days. We stopped for the night at the house of a disciple of Jesus. It was the first time we ever got to spend a lot of time alone with John. Mary had the idea that before Passover we should have a big dinner party for Jesus and Lazarus. John agreed. Mary also wanted to invite the mother of Jesus and Mary Magdalene. During the journey, we came up with many ideas for the party. This and my growing intimacy with Mary made the time go by quickly.

MARY: *When we arrived, it was an unusually somber gathering. Jesus had been teaching with many parables that were hard to understand. When he saw us, he began one about the death of Lazarus[86]. This radical parable, combined with Jesus's plan to enter Jerusalem for Passover, was unsettling.*

CLOPAS: And this is how it went. "There was a rich man who would dress in purple and fine linen, feasting lavishly every day. But a poor man named Lazarus, covered with sores, was left at his gate. He longed to be filled with what fell from the rich man's table, but instead the dogs would come and lick his sores. One day the poor man died and was carried away by the angels to the fold of Abraham's robe. The rich man also died and was buried. And being in torment in Hades, he looked up and saw Abraham a long way off with Lazarus at his side. 'Father Abraham!' he called out, 'Have mercy on me and send Lazarus to dip the tip of his finger in water and

---

[86] Luke 16:19-31

cool my tongue, because I am in agony in this flame!'

MARY: [In her lowest voice] "'You worthless one,' Abraham said, 'remember that during your life you received your good things, just as Lazarus received bad things, but now he is comforted here, while you are in agony. Besides all this, a great chasm has been fixed between us and you, so that those who want to pass over from here to you cannot; neither can those from there cross over to us.'"

CLOPAS: "'Father,' he said, "'Then I beg you to send him to my father's house-- because I have five brothers-- to warn them, so they won't also come to this place of torment.'"

But Abraham said,

MARY: "'They have Moses and the prophets; they should listen to them.'"

CLOPAS: "'No, father Abraham,' he said, "'But if someone from the dead goes to them, they will repent.'"

But he told him,

MARY: "'If they don't listen to Moses and the prophets, they will not be persuaded if someone rises from the dead.'"

CLOPAS: This shook me up. I had been thinking of Mary, of the party, of happy things. All that now seemed far away. I remembered all the bad things that had happened to me, Lazarus, and

Mary, while there were others, those few who seemed to live lives sheltered from suffering. Jesus's words often excited me, and I thought gleefully, "Finally some justice. They'll get their due! Anyone who knew of Lazarus's resurrection from the dead and lived their life as before would be punished, if not in this life, then the next!"

At this, Jesus looked at me, and I saw tears begin to form in his eyes. He continued,

MARY: *"It is impossible for causes of stumbling not to come, but woe to the one they come through! It would be better for him if a millstone were hung around his neck and he were thrown into the sea than for him to cause one of these little ones to stumble. Be on your guard. If your brother sins, rebuke him, and if he repents, forgive him. And if he sins against you seven times in a day and comes back to you seven times, saying,*

CLOPAS: 'I repent,'

MARY: *you must forgive him.[87]"*

I also had noticed Clopas's reaction. He got that look in his eye that scared me. It reminded me of our past and how often he'd twist Jesus's teachings to say what he wanted, not what Jesus had actually said. Had he changed at all? I had also been affected by the parable. Why did Jesus have to bring up Lazarus and death? I

---

[87] Luke 17: 1-4

did not want to be reminded that Lazarus would die again. Would I suffer like that again? Would I always be on my guard? Why couldn't Jesus let suffering pass us over? He knew I was wounded. Why reopen my wounds?

CLOPAS: The silence was awkward. Finally, we all said together, "increase our faith.[88]"

Jesus began to speak in parables again:

MARY: *"If you have faith like a mustard seed you can say to this mulberry tree, 'Be uprooted and planted in the sea,' and it will obey you.*

"Which one of you having a slave tending sheep or plowing will say to him when he comes in from the field,

CLOPAS: [haughty voice] " 'Come now and sit down to eat' "?

MARY: *"Instead, will he not tell him,"*

CLOPAS: [same voice] "'eat, tuck in your robe; later you can eat and drink'"?

MARY: *"Does he thank that slave because he did what was commanded? I don't think so! In the same way, when you have done all that you were commanded, you should say,"*

CLOPAS AND MARY: [like in meditation] **"'We are good-for-nothing slaves; we've only done our duty.'[89] "**

---

[88] Luke 17:5

[89] Luke 17:6-10

CLOPAS: [Laugh] This did not help me at the time. If anything I became more confused. Were we going to become enslaved? What was Jesus leading us into? Finally Jesus accepted our confusion and need to rest before we began our trek toward Jerusalem the next morning.

MARY: *As a woman and a former prostitute, I knew more about slavery than the men there. Jesus was talking about the need to accept a lower status in this world. But what did that mean for me?*

I still wanted the security and the status that would come from marriage. Even though I wanted to end my engagement with Judas, I knew there would be others. I still had my dowry and the disciples of Jesus seemed likely to forgive me for my past. And what of Clopas? Would I even consider him? Before Lazarus's death, he would have been the last man I would ever consider for a husband. But now I wasn't sure. I could maybe forgive him for his faults, including his pretensions. But Martha's voice haunted me. Clopas was what I "deserved" for a husband. Did I still think I deserved better? But wasn't that the point of Jesus's parable? We had to lower our status in this world to trust that God would provide. As I drifted off to sleep, I prayed for answers. . . .

CLOPAS: Early the next day we set off. Jesus was determined to go to Jerusalem, but he was not in a hurry. He took as many opportunities to teach us along the way as possible. There were so many places to do this, it took us four days to travel what normally took two.

MARY: *When we began, I finally got to talk with Judas. I told him I didn't want to marry him, but I didn't threaten him. For I remembered how my "god-father" had reacted when I threatened him. But Judas didn't want to end the engagement. He instead insisted that our contract of marriage be honored. He also tried to reconcile, but his entire manner was strange; he was nervous and jumpy. He wouldn't explain his absences from me other than that he had had to be with Jesus. But I couldn't believe him. His eyes betrayed him in the same way as when he told me he loved me. It convinced me of what I had held in denial for some time: he only wanted to marry me for my dowry. So I went to walk with Clopas instead.*

CLOPAS: I could tell she didn't want to talk about Judas so we talked about the party instead and anything else. By the end of the first day, we got to speak with Jesus about our desire to throw a party for him and Lazarus.

MARY: *He loved the idea. Things had been so serious, and we all needed a break. He even came up with the idea of having it at the house of a friend, a man named Simon who had had a serious skin disease. He knew that after the resurrection of Lazarus that the authorities were monitoring our house for signs of Jesus. He also had a favor to ask of us. Since the authorities were looking for him and we were not his usual disciples, he wondered if we could get something for him when we approached Bethphage and Bethlehem. We agreed.*

CLOPAS: The time passed quickly. Mary avoided Judas and walked with me. We talked about Jesus's teachings. Soon, as we approached Jericho, we were joined by a new former blind man[90]. He reminded me so much of myself when I first joined Jesus. We shared our story with him.

MARY: *Well parts of it. . . .*

CLOPAS: He also wanted a real name, like Clopas. I told him he could also be called Clopas, the other Clopas.

We three sat together at the house of Zacchaeus, or Zac, a chief tax collector. Zac had been trying to see who Jesus was, but he couldn't because of the crowd, since Jesus was a short man. So running ahead, he climbed up a sycamore tree to see Jesus, since he was about to pass that way. When Jesus came to the place, he looked up and said to him, "Zacchaeus, hurry and come down because today I must stay at your house.[91]"

The meal reminded me of when I first met Mary.

---

[90] **Luke 18:35-43**

[91] **Luke 19:1-5**

MARY: *I was also reminded of our first meeting, but this time it was different. I remembered how much Clopas had stared at me then and my first reaction to him. Now, I could see from the new Clopas that when a blind person first gets sight that they cannot help but stare at everything. The new Clopas, like my own Clopas, could not help but stare at me some. He could not help but talk more than the others. His entire life he'd been talking out to others. And who had included him in their conversations? A beggar is lower than a slave, for at least a slave is useful. . . . And any recently blind man would be full of things to say, as he takes it all in.*

CLOPAS: Like that first night, it proved to be eventful. Zac stood there and said to the Lord, "Look, I give half of my possessions to the poor, Lord! And if I have extorted anything from anyone, I pay back four times as much!" Jesus declared, MARY: *"Today salvation has come to this house because he too is a son of Abraham. For the Son of Man has come to seek and to save the lost.*[92]*"*

I thought, "Wow. He gave away his ill-gotten gains." It was as Jesus taught that night, what God had given us, we were responsible for and "to everyone who has, more will be given.[93]*" I left the house and went alone to pray, just like I had seen Jesus do so many times. After an hour of prayer, I made a decision: I would kill three birds with*

---

[92] Luke 19:8-10

[93] Luke 19:26

one stone. At the coming party, I would anoint Jesus again. This would let go of my ill-gotten gains, end my engagement with Judas, and show Jesus I believed he was the Messiah. For I remembered too well the groan that issued from Jesus when I questioned his love for Lazarus and me and his ability to raise him from the dead. I would lower my status by letting go of my chance to get married. For who would take a former prostitute without a dowry as a wife?

CLOPAS: Maybe . . . a former blind beggar?

[both laugh and hug]

CLOPAS: When Mary came back in, much later, there was joy in her eyes. I didn't know why then but I silently renewed my pledge to woo her. I was confident that there'd be time for both of us to fall in love. I was sure of it, just as I was sure that Jesus loved us both.

MARY: Yes, his wine spilled into both of our lives that night.

Mary's Second Anointing of Jesus, Fight with Martha and Adoption by Mary Mother of Jesus[94]

MARY: *The next day, we arrived at Mount Zion and Jesus told us, "Go, into the village ahead of you. As you enter it, you will find a young donkey tied there, on which no one has ever sat. Untie it and bring it here. If anyone asks you, 'Why are you untying it?' say this: 'The Lord needs it.'"*[95]

CLOPAS: So we left. I thought we might pretend we were a young couple, which she agreed to, and I loved. We strolled the streets and soon found what we'd come for. A hinny, the foal of a female donkey and male horse was tied there. This surprised us. However, as we began to untie it, its owners asked us, "Why are you untying the donkey?" We replied, "The Lord needs it."[96] They let us have him, but the hinny was so young, he did not want to leave his mother. So we asked and took both with us.[97] Each of us led an animal.

MARY: *And we got a few stares, since a hinny is unusual. It looks more like a horse than a donkey, but it's*

---

[94] based on John 12:1-11

[95] Luke 19:30-31

[96] Luke 19:32-34

[97] Matthew 21:7

as small as a donkey. However, nobody was going to give us any trouble for such a "useless" animal. It also gave me a chance to see how Clopas could focus. He could focus on encouraging the hinny along and then shift his focus to being friendly with those who passed by when prompted. It was another side of him for me. I found myself realizing that it was fun to talk with him, and he had a distinct, joyful laugh.

When I complimented him on his laugh, he remarked that he both laughed and cried with his whole heart, and then he looked away from me. We walked in silence. I had hurt him. I had hurt him when he had been trying so hard to get better. I saw how desperately he wanted to be worthy of me, but I had only seen him as a former blind beggar who couldn't adjust to normal life. We hurt each other so much sometimes.

CLOPAS: When we returned, Jesus received the hinny with joy, cheering both of us up. Jesus fed him, spoke with him, and rubbed his ears and back before he mounted him. I was amazed. They fit each other perfectly. Because Jesus was a small and gentle man, he was the only man who could have ridden the hinny colt, so young he still wanted his mother.

MARY: I would add that there was also a twinkle in Jesus's eyes when he saw us together. He wasn't just happy about the hinny. He was happy to see us together. And the twinkle remained in Jesus's eyes as he sent us off together again. For Mary Magdalene and Jesus had split our camp into two parts, one keeping camp near Mount Zion and the other to go into Bethany for the party. She had sent word to Simon to set up the party. Jesus and Mary took the hinny and his mother to the camp near Mount Zion, while Clopas and I went to get Martha and Lazarus, and others went to get supplies. We walked together slowly and did not talk.

CLOPAS: I did not know where to begin. When you care about someone who has hurt you a great deal, it is difficult to open up to them and be vulnerable. I did not want to destroy the tenuous relationship Mary and I had begun building, and I was afraid I would say or do something that would muddy the water between us again.

MARY: I thought about my engagement contract with Judas. I thought about Clopas. He had nothing. And then there was Jesus. What was going to happen? I knew what sort of leaders he threatened. They had tried to kill me. They would do the same to him. I had so many thoughts that I almost changed my mind about my final gift to Jesus.

CLOPAS: We arrived at Mary's home. Lazarus and Martha came out to greet us. We shared the good news and told some of the stories from our trip. Mary omitted the parable about Lazarus's death. We soon got lost in preparations, since it was six days before Passover, and we all had a lot to do. It was hard to prepare without others noticing our comings and goings.

MARY: *Lazarus was not a fast walker and easily recognized. How would we get to Simon's house without drawing a crowd with us? Clopas had an unusual idea.*

CLOPAS: What if we disguised Lazarus in a woman's clothing? We wrapped some of Mary's cloth around him tightly so Martha, Lazarus, and I could go together. He changed back at Simon's house.

MARY: *This worked. I told them I would catch up with them.*

CLOPAS: But Mary was late.

MARY: *People saw me and followed in an attempt to find Jesus. So I had to lead them along for awhile before I could slip away, losing them.*

CLOPAS: And, since the food was prepared, Martha appointed herself to serve us dinner. Jesus, Lazarus, Simon, Mary Magdalene, Jesus's mother, and some other disciples, including Judas (and myself of course), were all there and ate together. I wondered where Mary was when she appeared, in a simple dress this time. She walked quietly to where Jesus reclined. She had her alabaster vase with her so I thought I knew what she was doing, but then she surprised us all.

MARY: *I held my prize possession, my alabaster vase above Jesus. The first time I had kept it back with what was about one pound of fragrant oil, a pure and expensive nard. I had used a mere portion of it to entice Jesus into marriage with me, but this time I held nothing back. As I held it, I saw Martha's eyes widen, as she guessed what I was about to do. I froze as a voice like hers whispered in my mind, "there goes your only chance to get a decent husband." Our eyes locked as we knew what this meant for her. I didn't like risking the future of my brother and my sister, but it was my dowry. It was the wages of my sin, and I had provided for them from it for a long time. It was mine to give away.*

And since I believed Jesus was the Messiah, I also believed he would provide, somehow. He must've read my mind, because he nodded briefly. So I broke the vase and poured out the entire pound of nard on Jesus's head so that it spread down like a mist, anointing his whole body. It went all the way down to anoint his feet once again. So, once more, I fell to my knees, wiping his feet clean with my hair.

There were no tears this time. There was no need for them. I had no regrets over my actions. He had already forgiven my earlier lack of faith. Even more, I felt that with the nard came the release of all my regrets over my life of sin. I had stored them inside for so long. Now they'd been all transferred to Jesus.

CLOPAS: [Choked] It was a holy moment that only grew holier as the entire room soon was sanctified, bathed with the nard's earthy, musty scent. I felt it on myself and closed my eyes to breathe in deeply and soak it into my memory for forever. In my mind, the nard washed over me instead and transformed me into a new Clopas. One who attracted Mary as I was attracted to her.

What a complete immersion! Some nard landed on my lips, and I swirled it in my mouth. I had dreamt of what her nard might taste like; I had never tasted anything like it. It made my tongue burn like my eyes had burned. I lost myself in falling for Mary again, except this time, anticipation filled me instead of despair.

And then Judas barked in a nasally tone, "Why this waste? . . ." My eyes caught the blood gathering behind his face. He caught himself, his voice trickling off as he almost referred to the nard as his. Sweat dripped from his brow, mingling with the traces of nard before slipping onto his cloak. With his eyes clamped on Jesus who was similarly broken from a trance, Judas abruptly cleared his throat [clears throat] and began with his most scholarly tone, "Why wasn't this fragrant oil sold for many denarius and given to the poor?"

MARY: [laughs] *In another time or place, I'd have*

burst into laughter, but I was so immersed in that moment, I didn't give Judas's words any notice. My eyes, like my hopes for the future, were completely centered on Jesus.

CLOPAS: Thank God that the Iscariots' words of judgment didn't strike her again; history didn't repeat itself, but the essence of Jesus's response didn't change.

MARY: [imitates Jesus] *"Leave her alone; she has kept it for the day of my burial. For you always have the poor with you, but you do not always have me."*

CLOPAS: And right then, the poor, some of a large crowd of Jews who'd followed Mary, began to crowd in to see Jesus and Lazarus. For Lazarus had also begun to draw crowds. . . .

MARY: *Yes, and like me, they had begun to believe that Jesus really was the Messiah. I stood up, faced Judas, and slowly shook my head. I was not going to marry him. He looked from me to Jesus, and then he left us. Jesus looked at me with a sadness in his eyes right before he and Lazarus led the visitors who'd entered back outside. Clopas and other male disciples went with him, but the two other Marys and Martha remained with me. Then, my sister Martha drew me aside.*

She hissed, "What have you done? Are we both going to be prostitutes now? How are we to get married? Why did you reject Judas? He'd have made a great husband. He'd agreed to provide for all of us. And, what about

Lazarus? He can't support himself, especially if he goes around most of the time proclaiming Jesus as the Messiah! How can you care so little for your family?"

Her eyes were on the verge of tears. She meant every word. Now, I could have pointed out how the nard was my property. And I could have revealed why Judas would not have been a good husband. But I did not. I paraphrased Jesus, "who are my sister and my brother? Everyone who also follows Jesus is my sister or my brother.[98]" Martha, don't you see? Jesus is the Messiah and that's why I'm going to trust his promise that everyone who has left houses, brothers or sisters, father or mother, children, or fields because of his name will receive 100 times more and will inherit eternal life[99].

At this, her face grew red, especially since the other Marys heard us, and she practically shouted, "Are you claiming that I'm no longer your sister?" I replied, "I want to be your sister, but I've decided I must believe in Jesus. I denied him when Lazarus died. I've seen others give up their 'wealth'. It was my turn and I don't know what's going to happen. But everything I am now is because of him. What more could I have done for him? I want you to see why I did this. I want you to join me. Trust that Jesus, not some husband, will provide for all of us." Martha shook her head in disbelief. "How?" I could only reply, "I don't know."

It was a moment of truth. Martha made her choice. "It's just not right. Jesus was a great rabbi, but he's an even

---

[98] Matthew 12:48, 50

[99] Matthew 9:29

greater fool to come here now. And you are a fool to follow him. First you throw your dowry away for him, next you'll throw away the lives of your family for him. For Lazarus and I, we are your family. They're not my family. But now nobody's going to want to marry me, ever! You've ruined my life. Don't you ever come back to my house again!" And then she spun on her heel, crying as she left.

I wept.

Jesus's mother wrapped her arms around me. She said:

CLOPAS: [more feminine but not mocking voice] "You know when Jesus said those words about me, a sword pierced my own soul[100]. I have five sons and two daughters. . . . But they've now all gone their own ways. My daughters care only for their husbands. They resented Jesus. He didn't work as hard to earn as much as he could to help them to get good marriages. They blamed him for their modest dowries. John is going to be a Pharisee. Little Joseph, who reamed himself Josus to be like Jesus, now serves the Sadducees. Simon left for the Essenes, and my own Judas has left me to join the Zealots.

"And, oh, I wanted Jesus to stop him, to unite them all so we could be a family again. But not even Jesus can make people want to follow him.

---

[100] Luke 2:35

Mary, will you let me be your sister? Your family will be my family and your God, my son, will be my God[101]."

MARY: *It was another holy moment. Jesus's words became flesh, as Mary Magdalene joined us in an embrace. I do not know how long it lasted . . . but soon, it was time to go.*

CLOPAS: Jesus and I saw Martha leave crying. Jesus stopped, closed his eyes, and silently prayed. Then he told us it was time to go and motioned for me to get Mary. I came and found the three Marys, arms wound around each other. I did not want to disturb them, but I told them it was time to leave. We were to follow Jesus back to Mount Zion.

---

[101] **Ruth 1:16**

Clopas's Proposal, the Triumphal Entry, and the Second Death of Lazarus[102]

CLOPAS: On the way to Mount Zion, Mary walked with the women, and I walked with Lazarus. Lazarus understood everything about what had happened. He had long seen the "rift" widening between his sisters. It was only a matter of time and there was no question that he would come with us. We walked, and I told him that Mary's gift to Jesus was the most beautiful thing I had ever seen. He knew what I meant by that. He agreed with me and asked me to take care of her. This caught me. I stopped walking and looked him in the eyes. He was calm. Many thoughts flashed through my mind but none seemed right, except "I will."

So soon we arrived at the camp near Mount Zion. We all drew around Jesus. Some asked about the night, wondering why he was covered with nard. Jesus looked at Mary and then he looked at me.

MARY: [Jesus voice] *"Who would like to share the story?"*

CLOPAS: "I will, if it's okay with

---

102 based on John 12:12-19 and Luke 19:28-44

Mary."

MARY: *Clopas had come up a lot in my conversation with the other women. I had told them how much the death of Lazarus had affected me. When Judas was not there to support me in my grief, I fell out of love with him. Instead, it was Clopas who shared my anxiety and grief over Lazarus. I talked about our walk together with John to join Jesus. How I continued along with Clopas after Judas refused to end our engagement. How I continued to see Clopas differently when we were joined by our new friend who had just been healed of his blindness. How I was moved by Zacchaeus's promise to give my dowry to Jesus. How Clopas and I pretended to be a couple as we went to get the hinny. How things had become complicated as our old hurts rose within us. Needless to say, they liked him, and encouraged me to give "us" a chance. So when Clopas volunteered to tell my story, I said," Please do."*

CLOPAS: "In the beginning, I was saved by Jesus almost right after he saved Mary. When I first met Mary, I was sitting next to Jesus at a beautiful house, eating the best meal I had ever eaten and right then I met her, the most beautiful woman I had ever had the pleasure of beholding. Tonight was just like that. She came into the room, not for me, but for Jesus. She anointed Jesus's all, including his feet, with all of her nard, everything she had, and wiped his feet again with her hair. It made the room smell like

141

the temple. And I must admit . . . I fell in love with Mary again. I fell so hard that I am telling this story now so I can also ask her to marry me. Mary, will you marry me?"

MARY: *I was completely taken by surprise.* [Laughs] *I paused a little. I laughed some more because Clopas's proposal was so earnest—it sounded like it had just tumbled out of him. He was looking at me like he was going to explode, and I realized I hadn't answered him yet. "Yes! Yes, I will marry you, Clopas!" I exclaimed.*

CLOPAS: And I began to breathe again. It felt like I was in a dream. We had gone from a pretend couple to betrothed in one day. I grasped her hand, and we were applauded by all, including Mary Magdalene, who later promised to help us have a good wedding.

MARY: *Everyone was so happy for us. Jesus kissed us on both cheeks. The twinkle was back in his eyes, and I guessed he had known it was going to happen all along. There was a second, shorter engagement party, as we all began to get tired. Clopas asked Jesus about Judas's contract, wondering if we also needed a contract. Jesus told us that we need not worry about such things right then. And I prayed that night a prayer of thanksgiving for how God was continuing to bless me with new brothers and sisters*[103].

---

[103] Mark 10:29-30

The next morning came quickly. Jesus woke us all. We prayed, ate, and prepared to go. The hinny had been with his mother at the Mount Zion camp ever since we brought him the day before. But when Jesus spoke softly with him, the hinny was ready for him. Although, Jesus's mother led the hinny's mother on foot close behind so they could both gaze on their sons as they entered before a world that misunderstood them.

CLOPAS: I couldn't wait. The small king Jesus would enter Jerusalem on the smallest "horse," just as the "big" king Herod would enter on the biggest horse. Our world would be turned upside down, as Herod would be shown to be a false king. For he did not win his position by might, but by how he served the Romans. And he did not deserve to be king, because he served the Romans and himself far more than us.

MARY: *Jesus had told people last night that he would come into Jerusalem today from Mount Zion. And the news from last night had spread. We added to the drama, by putting our blankets and outer garments on the hinny colt for Jesus. This also contrasted with the fine things that Herod had stacked on his war-horse with him. The little fellow had never carried so much weight and went along slowly. The slowness of movement also mirrored Herod and his war horse.*

CLOPAS: Before we left, Jesus asked me to be his herald. No one was louder than me. I could call out his coming without the use of a horn. It was my time to shine. I would announce the coming of Jesus, as the King of Israel. I wanted Mary to come be with me so we could do it together.

MARY: *But I did not want to be in front. It's easy for Clopas to do that sort of thing because he is not easily distracted by crowds. He was used to drawing attention to himself, but I was much more modest. I didn't want to get that much attention. I wanted to stay in the back with Lazarus. Lazarus with his walking stick and our new friend, the other former blind man, were going to bring up the rear.*

CLOPAS: I didn't want to insist, but I did want her with me and so I told her that. Then Lazarus intervened saying, "Go with Clopas, Mary. Your place is with him. God will take care of us." For our new friend wanted to help Lazarus, like I used to help him. . . .

MARY: *And I did want to be with Clopas, so I accepted my position in front, however uncomfortable it made me. And so there we were, a former beggar and prostitute, heralding together the coming of King Jesus. Clopas went into his "court jester" mode where he completely focused on grabbing people's attention with loud proclamations of Jesus's coming. We held hands, waved palm branches, and we all proclaimed, "Hosanna! He who comes in the name of the Lord is the* blessed One--the King of Israel!" The crowd joined us in the cheer. They also grabbed palm branches and took their own cloaks off and spread them along the road for Jesus, mocking how we were made to greet the arrival of Herod into Jerusalem. It was an intense experience, but oh-so joyful. I had no problem just being there with Clopas. I did not think about what others thought of us or even about my brother. This continued throughout the morning; there were so many people that we proceeded rather slowly.

But as we got near to Jerusalem, some Pharisees stopped the march shortly to talk with Jesus. Around the same time, many of the Jews who witnessed the resurrection of Lazarus approached Clopas and I. While Jesus talked with the Pharisees, we stepped aside to talk with some of them. They inquired about Lazarus.

CLOPAS: Lazarus was on the lips of many. I understood why. A messiah who could raise his followers from the dead would have countless many willing to lay down their lives for him. God knows I had already been willing to do that for him. The sheer numbers of us and our willingness to die could maybe overcome the superior force of the Roman soldiers. This fantasy of mine was probably why I agreed to go get Lazarus so others could see him.

When I made my way to the back of our crowd, I had a hard time spotting him. Then, I saw their two bodies. The

former blind man who I thought would
also be the changing one, or called
Clopas, had fallen with his chin on
the ground, eyes and mouth open and a
puddle of blood leaked from his side.
Lazarus was to his left. He had the
most unusual look on his face given
that there was a small sword plunged
into his chest. He had fallen to his
knees and then backwards, head-first.
His eyes were closed, hands clasped
together as if he were in prayer.
Before him, Lazarus's stick was broken
in half. One of the Pharisees or their
servants had killed him, while the
others delayed the procession by
asking Jesus questions. Everyone else
was so focused on Jesus that no one
noticed. But why was the stick broken?

Now that they had accomplished their
goal, they had withdrawn so Jesus and
the others continued on the way. I
chose to tell Jesus about Lazarus
first. I guess I thought he might
bring them back to life to spare Mary
the grief from losing her brother
again and to give "Clopas" the same
chance at a new life that I had been
given. I went to him, whispering into
his ear as he leaned over to me. Upon
hearing about their murder, a tear
fell down his cheek. He quietly told
me to tell Mary and to take the bodies

back to the camp together.

Then he did the most unusual thing. He looked upon the city of Jerusalem and wept for it.

MARY: [Jesus voice] *"If you knew this day what would bring peace--but now it is hidden from your eyes. For the days will come on you when your enemies will build an embankment against you, surround you, and hem you in on every side. They will crush you and your children within you to the ground, and they will not leave one stone on another in you, because you did not recognize the time of your visitation."*[104]

CLOPAS: It was like his grief over the death of Lazarus and our new friend had spilled over to include a future grief when many would die, deaths that had just then seemed to become inevitable.

I did not and still do not understand this. But Jesus was like that, he defied what was normal. And, as a result of how he expressed his grief, the procession continued. I can imagine the Pharisees, maybe Simon and Judas Iscariot, said to one another, [evil voice] "You see? You've accomplished nothing. Look--the world has gone after him!"[105]

---

[104] Luke 19:41-44

[105] John 12:19

MARY: *My life spun around again. Clopas and I wept together silently, as we wrapped my brother and our new friend in some of the robes that had been left on the ground. We each took one side and carried Lazarus back to camp. As we walked, I eventually said what had been on my mind. "I should have been back there with him. . . . Why did Jesus not resurrect him again?"*

CLOPAS: I replied, "Don't say that. If you had been with him, they might have killed you. I don't know why Jesus did not resurrect him, I suppose he still could. But I didn't understand what Jesus did the first time Lazarus died either. There's got to be a reason."

MARY: *And even though I felt my grief rising up, it did not overwhelm me. I was changed. I remembered Jesus's words about the future destruction of Jerusalem. They helped me to see Lazarus's second death differently. Lots of lives were at stake, and Jesus gave no promise that we would not suffer and die. He had not promised to resurrect us in the here and now. So I replied, "Maybe it was his time. . . . Jesus did tell us that story about Lazarus in heaven. He might have told it to prepare us for this. I mean, all those people, all they talked about was Lazarus's resurrection."*

CLOPAS: "Yes, if Jesus raised him from the dead again that's all they would talk about. . . . It's almost like it was a test. They wanted to see if he would raise Lazarus from the dead again. They're just like the family of that rich man in the parable. They'd only repent if someone from the dead goes to them."

MARY: *"But Abraham said,'if they don't listen to Moses and the prophets, they will not be persuaded if someone rises from the dead.' I think I understand that but my heart still tells me I should have been with him."*

CLOPAS: "But you were with me. I am your family now. We're going to get married."

MARY: *"Yes, but my heart must weep some more. You understand this, do you not? He was my brother, and I loved him." Then we arrived back in the camp where Jesus's mother and Mary Magdalene joined us in weeping for Lazarus, as we all hugged, ripped our clothing, and sat together on the ground to weep some more without words. Then, Mary Magdalene and Clopas went back to get our friend, and so the mother of Jesus let me rest my head on her bosom and weep some more. Much later Jesus and the others returned. When they arrived at the temple complex, Jesus went into it but it was too late, so they came back*[106].

We had a funeral for Lazarus and the new Clopas. Jesus spoke simply of his love for Lazarus, reassuring us that it was their time to be with the Father in heaven. Clopas spoke of how happy Lazarus had been since his resurrection and how many people who had believed because of him. He also spoke of "Clopas" and how much he had wanted to witness and help make similar changes

---

[106] **Mark 11:11**

happen in his new friend's life. I told about how long and hard Lazarus had prayed for me. It was because of his prayers that I was with them. I shared about how the new Clopas's joy and enthusiasm had helped me to see my own Clopas with new eyes that held more joy and enthusiasm. Others spoke. Martha had been invited but did not come.

CLOPAS: It was a bitter ending to an exhausting day. We retired early, and Jesus spent time alone in prayer.

How Things Almost Fell Completely Apart

CLOPAS: The next morning Jesus led us back to the temple complex. He entered, his face red and eyes flaming, throwing out those who were selling there as if they had been the ones who ordered the murder of Lazarus, saying,

MARY: *"It is written, my house will be a house of prayer, but you have made it a den of thieves!*[107]*"*

CLOPAS: As I described before, this and the murder of Lazarus unleashed my zealot enthusiasm. It was time for Justice!

MARY: *Meanwhile, I, just like the night before, was plagued with doubts in my heart. The words of my sister Martha came back. I had deserted her and Lazarus. It was my fault that they were hopeless or dead. It raised doubts about Clopas. "Was it right to get engaged to him right after the end of my engagement with Judas? We were so different. The day before had gone well at first, but then death had struck back. And Clopas's reaction to Jesus's cleansing of the temple made it clear how different we were."*

I would not have gone with them if Clopas had not insisted. And I know Jesus used the whip on the animals, not the money-changers, but it still was violence, and I knew violence led to more violence. How was it going to

---

[107] Luke 19:45-6

end? How can two radically different people get married in a world about to fall apart? Wouldn't we just drive each other into madness?"

Like Clopas and like everyone, I was so full of emotions. Clopas did legitimately add to my distress, but he was more a convenient scapegoat. And I hurt him with my doubts. I rubbed salt on some old wounds of his and reopened a rift between us.

CLOPAS: I was arrested by vivid images, and the corpses of Lazarus and the new Clopas were no exception. I had never seen so much blood before. I found I couldn't describe it very well. Death had not been visual for me, just theoretical. I also had never witnessed anything like Jesus whipping the money-changers' things. I need help to rebalance my life, since I easily burn with zeal. The spark ignites in my heart and spreads within me. I burn so much that I resent others who do not similarly want to spread a zeal for "Justice" in the moment. When Mary reacted as she did to the temple cleansing, I began to burn with resentment towards her. We grew even more disconnected. We didn't immediately end our engagement, but we were both in agony over:

CLOPAS AND MARY: **Had we been too hasty in coming together?**

CLOPAS: I wasn't the only one who got

excited about Jesus after he cleansed the temple a second time. Passover would have been the perfect time to start a Jewish rebellion and the other occupied groups in the Roman Empire knew it. The memories of past freedom from oppressive rule were at their strongest. And the timing of a rebellion mattered. This is why some Greeks were among those who went up to worship at the festival. When they heard of Jesus, they judged rightly that he was their best bet for who could start a rebellion in Jerusalem at Passover. The people were behind him more than anyone else. He was the one to unite the Jews in a rebellion so powerful that it would free other groups to start their own rebellions. While the Roman army could easily put down a single rebellion within the Empire, it would struggle if it had to put down two at the same time. And if it struggled with crushing both rebellions then more rebellions elsewhere were sure to arise. All together they could bring an end to the Roman Empire. This was the hope of the Zealots. And the ideas of the Zealots were known by Jesus and his followers, for about half of his followers, not just Simon the Zealot, had long held strong Zealot sympathies.

So when the Greeks contacted Philip, I was onboard, as I happened to be there. It was obvious what they wanted. They must have heard about Jesus's cleansing of the temple. They wanted to talk with Jesus about whether he would ignite a rebellion in Jerusalem on Passover so they could do the same in their part of Greece. Philip went and told Andrew, another strong Zealot sympathizer. Then, they both went and told Jesus, while I tagged along[108].

Jesus knew what we wanted. Our fervor for change had grown and intensified. This was a chance that would never repeat itself. Jesus responded by backing away from us and the Greeks. He then replied to us in a loud voice,

MARY: [imitates Jesus] *"The hour has come for the Son of Man to be glorified[109]."*

CLOPAS: This got everyone's attention, and as many gathered around Jesus, the Greeks were obviously uncomfortable.

MARY: [imitates Jesus] *"I assure you: Unless a grain of wheat falls to the ground and dies, it remains by itself. But if it dies, it produces a large crop. The one who loves his life will lose it, and the one who hates his life in this world will keep it for eternal life. If anyone serves me, he*

---

[108] John 12:20-22
[109] John 12:23

must follow me. Where I am, there my servant also will be. If anyone serves me, the Father will honor him.

"Now my soul is troubled. What should I say--Father, save me from this hour? But that is why I came to this hour. Father glorify your name![110]"

CLOPAS: And then a voice came from the sky: [deep voice] "I have glorified it, and I will glorify it again!" It caught us by surprise. Many there said it was just thunder.

MARY: Others said an angel had spoken to Jesus[111].

CLOPAS: It went over my head, as Jesus's resounding "no" to the Zealot cause echoed in my mind.

MARY: I didn't know about the Greek Zealots' attempt to meet Jesus, so Jesus's speech was a surprise for me. I did not understand it then. What interested me was Clopas's reaction to it. He was listening to Jesus intently like usual, but his shoulders were slumped and his face downcast in anxiety and disappointment. It was the same posture he'd usually have after his failed attempts to woo me. To see him like this again frightened me.

His earlier excitement over Jesus's cleansing of the temple had reminded me how different our worlds were. My family, like most Jews with some property, had feared the Zealots. We had turned to the Pharisees for inspiration from the Torah for nonviolent ways to

---

[110] John 12:24-28a

[111] John 12:28b-29

change the Roman empire. We paid them, and they gave us ideas and some leadership, but they often promoted themselves more than they helped us. But before Jesus, we didn't have much of a choice. It was basically either them or the Zealots and the massive death and destruction they would bring.

CLOPAS: Is it any wonder with these options that there had been such deep longings for the Messiah? Is it any wonder that so many false messiahs sprang up from all manner of places?

MARY: Jesus continued to interact with the crowd, slowly moving in the opposite direction of the Greeks. Right after he finished a bizarre response to the question of "who is this Son of Man?" he left and went and hid from the Greeks[112]. And I felt like Jesus was on my side, the Anti-Zealot side. He also was afraid for his life.

CLOPAS: We went with Jesus to one of our safe spots in Jerusalem. I remember the look on the faces of the Greeks when it was clear that Jesus wanted nothing to do with them. It was no different than the look on Simon Iscariot's face when Jesus turned his back on him.

And, I see now that collaboration with the Greek rebels would have ruined everything. Jesus was right to fear

---

[112] John 12:36

them because they'd kill anyone who might ruin their mission. That's the sort of commitment that Zealots had to have to their cause. Their zeal for their cause upset the rest of their lives, just as Mary was upset with me.

We had already had a short fight after the cleansing of the temple. She was against any use of violence. She wanted to wait and see what Jesus would do about the Roman Empire. She believed he'd find a third way without any violence. I was gripped by how much I wanted an end to the Roman Empire.

I couldn't imagine God letting things get worse than they already were. What's the point of believing in God, but living our lives afraid of all violence? Besides, I knew that there was plenty of violence already for most of us sinners, or common folk, but for those like Mary or Judas, whose families cooperated with Rome, violence was something they had been spared. Their opposition to "violence" was not carried out against the violence that we sinners often faced!

MARY: *Jesus sensed the warring ideologies at work between Clopas and me. He asked both of us to come with him. We followed him. Not far away, he stopped and turned around and held our hands separately.*

[They hold out their hands as if they were held by Jesus. Mary imitates Jesus] *"You two are very different in many ways. This is a good thing."*

CLOPAS: [imitates Jesus] "For God created us Man and Woman,"

MARY: [imitates Jesus] *different and yet the same."*

CLOPAS: [imitates Jesus] "You both see in part, but you see different parts.

MARY: [imitates Jesus] *"This is why my father gave both of you to me at the same time. You are meant to be together. You both love me and you share the same passion. You share a passion that comes from my father. It is meant to be a gift for you both, as well as a gift for others. But any passion can become a curse."*

CLOPAS: [imitates Jesus] "Clopas, your life has been hard from the very beginning. You've had to beg for basic needs that my father meant for all of humanity to have met. Yet, you did more than beg, you listened. You listened to the cries of many. You saw how how bad things are, even before you could see. And you continue to change as you walk towards the light. You truly want things to get better, but you remain blind to how things could get much worse. You let the ideas that bloom in your imagination cover up your eyes. You do not see how much of the affairs of this world are a pursuit of the wind[113]. You love an illusion of greatness. You use it to avoid facing how our lives are only a vapor[114]. This is not the way for a husband to be! Please, let Caesar be and trust God to be God."

MARY: [imitates Jesus] *"And Mary, you deserve a husband who will love you, who will forsake all other ties or callings to bond with you. You, like many women, have suffered due to how perverse our world has become. You also have seen humiliation and death's shadow. And you have let go of your treasure. This has given you strength and wisdom."*

CLOPAS: [imitates Jesus] "But your love of others must grow deeper. You're still struggling with fears of your future. These very fears blind you to the many sorrows of others. Clopas will help you, as you will help him. Please forgive him when he stumbles back into a pit that has trapped him before. He will need you to continue to follow me."

MARY AND CLOPAS: [imitating Jesus] ***"And so, I love you both, let me love you to the end[115]. This Wednesday evening would be a ripe time to get married, for I fervently desire to rejoice over your marriage. I will not rejoice***

---

[113] Ecclesiastes 1:14

[114] Psalm 62:9a

[115] John 13:1b

again in that way until the kingdom of God comes[116]**."**

MARY: *And with that, Jesus drew our hands together.* [They hold hands.] *Clopas asked me to marry him, and I accepted again. We went back inside and announced that our wedding would be tomorrow night. This brought back the new wine that had ran out with the death of Lazarus and the conflict over the Greek rebels among the followers of Jesus.*

---

[116] Luke 22:18

A Wedding and a Seder

MARY: *Most of us headed back to camp to begin the wedding plans, but Jesus went back to the temple and continued his mission there until it was evening[117]. He would do the same thing the next day and even the day of our wedding. Although, on the night before, he committed himself to prayer about how he would shepherd our wedding. And, once more, he turned the ordinary into the finest, so that our joy would spill over to many.*

CLOPAS: It was amazing! I went with Jesus to the temple, at the request of Mary. [Both Laugh]

MARY: *Clopas wanted to help, but we knew he'd be more likely to get in the way.*

CLOPAS: It was a blessing. Jesus's words to us remained in my mind. I had never felt closer to him before. You'd think that my thoughts would have been all about Mary, but Jesus reigned over her in them. I had thought about Mary [laughs] a lot in the past. This was different. A storm within me had been quieted. I wanted nothing else but to be with him, to hear his voice, and to see his face.

MARY: *At first, my thoughts went to Clopas. I envied his time to "sit at Jesus' feet" as we became busy with the many tasks that had to be done in little time. But I*

---

[117] Luke 21:37

accepted that this was his time to be with Jesus. And soon we lost ourselves in preparations, just like Clopas lost himself in Jesus, or as Jesus's mother had lost herself in her search for the lost coin.

The most important thing we had to decide was the location for the wedding. We didn't want another crowd to disrupt us so we needed a secure place. Mary Magdalene suggested that we go to a garden that was in the Kidron valley. It was a garden where Jesus and his followers had met many times. It also was, unknown to us, the same garden where Jesus would be arrested on Thursday evening[118].

And thankfully, we pulled everything together in time for Wednesday night. Then, as Jesus, Clopas, and I walked to the garden, I grew nervous because I had not ended my official betrothal to Judas. . . .

CLOPAS: Fortunately, Jesus had a plan if Judas caused any trouble.

MARY: Yes. And as we were walking Clopas sweetly and shyly said to Jesus . . .

CLOPAS: Jesus, I have no dowry to offer Mary. I have always been poor, though in truth I am as rich as the lilies of the field.

MARY: [Jesus voice] "Clopas, you are right. You have begun to learn that all you need will be provided. You should consider your personal sacrifice for Lazarus as your dowry."

---

[118] John 18:1

[Own voice] *To which I added, "I couldn't ask for a greater dowry than when you ran day and night to get Jesus to save my brother. You laid down your life for my brother, there's no greater love than that*[119]. *And, I also didn't thank you yet for how you saved my life. If you had not invited me to be at your side, crying out praises for Jesus as he entered into Jerusalem, then they would have killed me along with my brother. Thank you, Clopas."*

CLOPAS: I felt at peace hearing those words. We entered the garden, not knowing how Jesus would unite us in marriage. When we came to the place he had chosen, he made a canopy of a linen cloth, just like one that might be used for Yom Kippur . . .

MARY: *or a burial. And then Jesus invited us under the canopy. He said, "Today you are united in my name." He called his mother and Mary Magdalene forward and said, "Today we are celebrating a new family: a new humanity."*

CLOPAS: And, I thought, wait I have no ring. Isn't there supposed to be more to this? What about the contract to sign? And then as if he'd read my thoughts Jesus said,

MARY: [Jesus voice] *"My spirit will bind you together. Your union will be written in your hearts. We need no contracts and payments among us at this time."*

---

[119] **John 15:13**

CLOPAS: He then turned to Judas. Judas had come uninvited. He was dressed as if he were in Herod's court. Who knows what plan lurked in his mind? He could have led the authorities to get Jesus that night, but maybe he still thought he could force Mary to marry him instead, since they had an engagement contract. "Friend, your garment of blood and deceitful words have no place here." Upon hearing those words, Judas turned away and left.

MARY: *Without pause, Jesus announced, "What God has joined together, let no man separate![120]"*

And then he turned back to us and raised a glass of wine in blessing. He started with the blessing over the wine as the first of the seven blessings for our marriage:

"Blessed are You, Adonai, our God, King of the universe, Creator of the fruit of the vine.

"Blessed are You, Adonai, our God, King of the universe, who has created everything for your glory.

"Blessed are You, Adonai, our God, King of the universe, Creator of human beings.

CLOPAS: "Blessed are You, Adonai, our God, King of the universe, who has fashioned human beings in your image, according to your likeness and has fashioned from it a lasting mold. Blessed are You, Adonai, Creator of

[120] **Mark 10:9**

human beings.

"Bring intense joy and exultation to the barren one [Jerusalem] through the ingathering of her children amidst her in gladness. Blessed are You, Adonai, who gladdens Zion through her children.

"Gladden the beloved companions as You gladdened Your creatures in the garden of Eden. Blessed are You, Adonai, who gladdens groom and bride.

MARY AND CLOPAS: *"Blessed are You, Adonai, our God, King of the universe, who created joy and gladness, groom and bride, mirth, glad song, pleasure, delight, love, brotherhood, peace, and companionship. Adonai, our God, let there soon be heard in the cities of Judah and the streets of Jerusalem the sound of joy and the sound of gladness, the voice of the groom and the voice of the bride, the sound of the grooms' jubilance from their canopies and of the youths from their song-filled feasts. Blessed are You who causes the groom to rejoice with his bride."*

CLOPAS: And then he added, "This glass is my blood which flows for the world. By it you are united and all will be united together." And then he gave us the glass to drink. After we had finished drinking from it he drank the small amount left and shattered the glass on the ground.

MARY: *We both wondered in our hearts what this meant and then again he spoke aloud and answered our unspoken question . . .*

MARY AND CLOPAS: **"This temple will be destroyed and rebuilt. By it all will be blessed. Amen."**

MARY: *And then we all sang and sang and there was dancing and rejoicing. And then Jesus told us to stay in the garden and sleep under the canopy. . . .*

CLOPAS: And we were husband and wife.

[Pause, as they hold hands together and look into each other's eyes.]

How beautiful you are, my darling.

How very beautiful!

Your eyes are doves.

MARY: *How handsome you are, my love.*

How delightful!

Our bed is lush with foliage;

the beams of our house are cedars,

and our rafters are pines[121]

CLOPAS: We slept late, ate well, and enjoyed this new way of being together. If only I enjoyed life with the wife I love for all the days of my fleeting life as much as I did on that

---

[121] **Song of Solomon 1:15-17**

day[122].

MARY: *Too soon, it was time for us to join Mary Magdalene, Jesus's mother, and others for a Passover meal.*

CLOPAS: And as always Jesus gave us surprise after surprise.

MARY: *He said we were to celebrate the Passover in Bethany.*

CLOPAS: And not Jerusalem where the law required us to be. I thought to myself that it was not lawful to even leave the greater Jerusalem area on the night of the Passover. Pilgrims come from all over the world to be in the city and we would leave it? It was a shock. Wouldn't we be with him in the city?

MARY: *I had similar thoughts, and again Jesus answered our thoughts before we could speak them. He said,*

CLOPAS: [Jesus voice] "The deliverance I give is not bound by any city walls. Celebrate in spirit and truth, live the reality of the exodus: true worship and liberation." And then he added,

MARY: [Jesus voice] *"Clopas, you will head the table in my place for I will be in Jerusalem with my apostles to*

---

[122] **Ecclesiastes 9:9**

set the table for what I must give."

CLOPAS: My mind reeled and my heart swelled with the joy and honor that I would be the father of a Passover celebration. I, a former blind beggar, was now not only married, I was going to celebrate my deliverance, *our* deliverance, as head of a family, a family Jesus, the Messiah, had brought together.

MARY: *I was so proud and full of joy too. Both Mary Magdalene and Jesus's mother smiled and said, "let us go...."*

CLOPAS: All is prepared.

MARY: *And we all laughed and laughed when I asked, "How is this night different than all other nights?"* [Both laugh]

CLOPAS: Yes, it was a deep mix of gravity and joy. At the beginning, we drank the first cup to celebrate our physical freedom. I cried out in thanks, full of wonder over my restored new life because of Jesus; now I could raise the glass and look on my beloved.

MARY: *I too wept at the joy of the physical freedom Jesus had given me. I would never again be a slave to any man's desires. Instead, I'd been given a choice, and I would only give of myself to the man I loved, my partner.*

CLOPAS: And each part was so real, so

personal for us: As individuals, and
as a couple, and. . . .

MARY: *as part of the people of God.*

*Yes, this included the bitterness of the bitter herbs. It
brought back the memory of all the bitter times. . . .*

CLOPAS: The matzo also brought powerful
memories: the bread of suffering, for
we had suffered greatly so
recently. . . . But Passover tradition
kept these memories brief so they did
not overwhelm.

MARY: *Instead, we were able to retell the miracles of
our people and their deliverance from slavery in Egypt.
These old stories became more real for us all. They added
flavor to all we had experienced in Jesus. . . .*

CLOPAS: And all we hoped to experience
with Jesus and each other.

Each of the four cups we drank made
real what Jesus had done. With the
second and third cup, we celebrated
the freedom of the mind and our
spiritual freedom. It made me laugh. I
saw how my pride and anger had kept me
blind.

MARY: *And I laughed at how I used to despise Clopas,
instead admiring Judas. To think, Judas!*

CLOPAS: On the fourth cup, we were all
silent. Our mood was deep with wonder.
We celebrated our partnership with
God. For we knew we had parts to play

in the way God was at work in our midst.

MARY: *And, of course, we all thought of Jesus.*

CLOPAS: Never had I felt such joy and wonder all at once.

MARY: *Time stood still in that moment and it was like we were all looking down on ...*

CLOPAS: the Promised Land. And we sang and sang with joy. And we went to sleep without any cares or concerns on our hearts.

MARY: *Only the joy of our love and the light of Jesus in our lives.*

[Silence]

In the Shadow of the Cross

CLOPAS: And then Peter came, not long after the rooster crowed. He had not slept at all. He was a mess—hair askew, eyes red-rimmed. We got out of him that Judas had betrayed Jesus with a kiss to Caiaphas for thirty pieces of silver. And now Jesus was being taken before the governor. There was only one reason Jewish leaders would take a prisoner to the Roman officials: they wanted the death penalty. And I knew they would get it!

MARY: *Our bubble burst. Clopas reacted first.*

CLOPAS: I asked Peter for his small sword and then asked Mary to tell me how to find the field that Judas had wanted to buy for thirty pieces of silver.

Peter had two small swords. One was John's, who had given Peter his when John went into the high priest's courtyard[123]. He was glad to hand them both over to me, for they had brought him only misery. Peter staggered away, weeping over Jesus and how he had failed him.

Meanwhile, Mary was stewing.

---

[123] **John 18:15-16**

MARY: *I couldn't believe he wanted to go after Judas. Clopas isn't a fighter. The night before I had told Clopas everything I could about Judas and me. I told him that Judas had taken me to a potter's field, explaining what Judas had shared with me about why he wanted to buy the field. Clopas asked me if I could find my way back to the field, and I told him I was sure of it. But I thought that was something we would do much later, along with many other followers of Jesus. Clopas wanted to go after Judas alone with two small swords. What did he expect to do upon finding Judas, best him with a sword?*

Clopas was burning with righteous indignation, and I loved him. But I had hoped this zealotry was behind us after our time with Jesus.

[Both step forward and into the past facing each other. Hands on her hips, Mary talks to Clopas.] *"It doesn't matter what Judas did to Jesus, we're supposed to turn the other cheek. . . . And what if he killed you? I know about your "sword lessons" from Judas. The bruises on you were impossible to hide. It's suicidal to attack a better swordsman with small swords. They're only meant for self-defense.* [shakes head] *There's no way I am going to help you get killed doing the wrong thing. . . ."*

CLOPAS: "But what about Jesus? He saved us both. Judas betrayed him. He's betrayed us. I mean, was it by chance that the murderer of Lazarus had broken his staff? That was an unnecessary, personal act. It was what we should expect from Judas, especially after he'd just been shamed

172

by your rejection of him.

"From the beginning, I had been right about him. He should be sent to Sheol. Perhaps it is up to me to send him there? And why expect the worse? Isn't God on our side? Why wouldn't God deliver Judas to me, like God delivered Goliath to David? Judas has turned his back on Jesus. He's going to preach a perverted form of Jesus's good news from the synagogue he's going to build in this field. Are we going to just let him get away with it?

"I mean of *all* of Jesus's followers, Peter has had the most spunk, and now he's crying like a baby. If not us, who else will seize the moment to act while Judas's guard is down?"

MARY: *"But we are followers of Jesus. This is not the way Jesus has shown us. It's the same path that almost destroyed our relationship before. Jesus loved us, he brought us back together. 'What God has joined together, let no man separate!' We can't let Judas separate us, we're joined together!"*

CLOPAS: "Everything's about relationships with you. What about Justice? Is there nothing to you worth dying for? If Judas lives and succeeds then they'll laugh at Jesus and all that he stood for. He'll be just another failed 'messiah'. . . .

I need you to support me on this. Have faith in God and me. Please, if you love me tell me how to get to Judas's potter's field. I promise you I will never use a sword ever again."

MARY: "When Judas kills you, you'll never use a sword ever again, you foolish man! You're asking me to help you murder Judas. Don't you see how wrong that is? You're saying I don't love you unless I give you what you want.

How can you do that to me? I do love you, but I hate this. I hate the way you're manipulating me. Didn't you hear what Jesus said to you about how much of life is a chasing after of the wind? Let God be God, God will render unto Judas what he deserves! How can you say you love me and use my love for you like this? That's not love, that's blindness!"

CLOPAS: "I'm blind? What if I'm God's tool for rendering Judas to Sheol? I've hated Judas from the beginning. Every minute when he taunted me while pretending to teach me the sword, I couldn't help but imagine that someday it might come down to this. I didn't know how, I just knew. I know I'm not a swordsman, but I am not a lot of things, and that's never stopped me.

I probably wasn't the right one to go to tell Jesus about Lazarus dying, but with God's help I did it. I did it, and God used it to bridge the gulf between us. This could be just like that. God will grace me with what is needed. You don't think Judas deserves to live, do you? What if he also killed Lazarus?"

MARY: *"Does Judas deserve to live? Is God going to use you to strike him down? Who am I to answer these questions? No, Judas deserves to die. But I don't see why your past hatred of Judas gives you the right to kill him. It's still murder. Even if Judas had killed Lazarus, it doesn't justify you taking his life."*

CLOPAS: "But it's *not* murder. Jesus does not deserve to die, but Judas does, especially if he murdered Lazarus. We both know this. If we don't take action now, the whole establishment will protect Judas so he can subvert Jesus's teachings to their ends! You know Judas; you know how crafty these people are. If we don't do something now then who will? Like I said, I'm asking you as your husband to submit to me on this. Tell me how to get to the field Judas planned to buy! *Please!*"

[Silence, Clopas hangs his head in remorse. They step back and Mary faces the audience again.]

MARY: [sighs] *I agreed, but with a heavy heart. When Clopas leaned in to kiss me, I would not let him, and it was in this manner that we parted ways.*

I went with the other women to get some of the other supporters of Jesus. We desperately wanted to know what Pontius Pilate had to say. We did not expect justice. Rome was and is, above all else, about stability. Jesus was the opposite of stability; he was about true change, the change that can only come from the bottom-up, never the top-down. And so there were no surprises when the powers-that-be did and said what they felt was necessary; they sent Jesus to the cross.

Even though we knew what was coming, we were still in shock. Some, like me, were waiting for a miracle to happen in the last moment. But such a belief was hard to hold. It just didn't make sense. Rome was too good at killing people. As Jesus made his way to his execution, some of us wept, lamenting his brutal end. Jesus had been whipped so much that his flesh hung in bloody ribbons from his body. His once strong arms struggled to carry his own cross. Any other man forced to carry a heavy cross after being whipped so much would have died well before reaching the hill of execution. Jesus heard us crying behind him and recognized our voices. He turned to us and said,

CLOPAS: [imitating Jesus] "Daughters of Jerusalem, do not weep for me, but weep for yourselves and your children. Look, the days are coming when they will say, 'The women without children, the wombs that never bore and the breasts that never nursed are fortunate!' Then they will begin to say to the mountains, 'Fall on us!' and to the hills, 'Cover us!' For if they do these things when the wood is green, what will happen when it is dry?[124]"

[Clopas stretches his arms out as if they were nailed on a cross.]

MARY: [Kneels on ground looking up and then turns to audience] *We wept for Jesus. I wept for Jesus and Clopas. For all I knew I'd sent Clopas to his death as well. Jesus's mother, Mary Magdalene, and I stood huddled before Jesus's cross in agony over his suffering[125]. John had joined us. It was just us few near the cross. The other women supporters of Jesus stood at further distance watching these things[126]. Without the strength of Jesus's mother, I couldn't have endured the terrible mixture of being so close to Jesus's immense suffering and wondering when God would intervene. I wondered how on earth she could endure it. How could it be that she was the one holding me up? She was my sister, as I was hers[127]. We waited for the kingship of God to be shown before us all. But instead, Jesus, looking down on us, made it clear that he was about to die. He dulled the pain for us as his blood-stained eyes met ours. He spoke in a raspy voice with arms stretched out as if in a caress to the woman who had borne him.*

CLOPAS: [still with his arms outstretched] "Woman, here is your son."

---

[124] Luke 23:28-31

[125] John 19:25

[126] Luke 23:49

[127] John 19:25

MARY: *And then to John.*

CLOPAS: [imitates Jesus] "Here is your mother."[128]

MARY: *After this, when Jesus knew that everything was now accomplished that the Scripture might be fulfilled, he said,*

CLOPAS: "I'm thirsty!"

MARY: *A jar full of sour wine was sitting there: so they fixed a sponge full of sour wine on hyssop and held it up to his mouth.*[129]

When Jesus had received the sour wine, he said,

CLOPAS: "Father, into your hands I entrust my spirit. [Breathing out] It is finished."[130]

[Clopas bows his head.]

[Silence. Clopas steps back into narrator mode.]

He died at the time when the Passover lamb would have been slain. I missed it. [Sighs] Instead of following Jesus to the cross, I went my own way, consumed with thoughts of Judas. I was so obsessed with revenge that I was almost run over by a chariot. As my life flashed before me, I remembered how God had provided before and began

---

[128] John 19:26-27a

[129] John 19:28-29

[130] John 19:30, Luke 23:46

to pray without ceasing, "Jesus, guide me!" as I followed Mary's directions.

MARY: *I also was praying without ceasing, "Jesus, calm me."*

CLOPAS: When I got to the field, Judas and his father had just arranged the purchase. But there were too many people. I would pray and wait for Judas to return.

MARY: *Clopas had been right. They planned to subvert the Jesus movement by elevating Judas as the greatest of his disciples. They were practically giving him his own synagogue from which he could interpret Jesus's teachings "correctly." I'm sure if Clopas had not gone after Judas that God would have acted in some other way, but instead God intervened so I wouldn't be separated from the two great loves of my life, Jesus and Clopas.*

CLOPAS: As I asked Jesus to guide me, I came to see that Mary was right. I was the last person to kill or murder anyone. But I also saw that I had three options: I could go back to Mary. I could trust that God would save the day somehow. Or, I could turn my weakness into a strength. But how does one turn a weakness with the sword into a strength? Judas wouldn't fear me, could that be an advantage? I remembered my time with Jesus and how he loved me. I prayed, "Jesus guide me" and my mind traced over Scripture, looking for the word for the moment. I did this until he kindled a flame that I tended until it was time.

MARY: *Our flame was also kept alive when a "good Samaritan" came to our help. He was Joseph of Arimathea. He was a member of the Sanhedrin who had not agreed with their plan and action. Like I did, Joseph was willing to sacrifice his wealth for Jesus. He approached Pilate with a bribe and asked for Jesus's body. Taking it down from the cross, he wrapped it in fine linen and paid top dollar to place it in a nearby tomb cut into the rock, where no one had ever been placed. It was preparation day, and the Sabbath was about to begin[131].*

He let us follow along and observe the tomb and how Jesus's body was placed. Then we returned and spent the rest of preparation day working through our grief together. With the generous help of Joseph, we prepared our best once more for Jesus. We prepared spices and perfumes until it was sundown, and then we rested on the Sabbath according to the commandment[132].

That Sabbath was full of memories of Jesus. We women followers of Jesus shared our best of him. We were blessed with tears and awe. He had deeply touched each of our lives – treating us as equals instead of property. It was the wine we'd expected from the true king. But with his death, we wondered if that wine would sour. Would the

---

[131] Luke 23:50-54

[132] Luke 23:55-56

other male followers of Jesus continue to follow his example, treating us as peers? We didn't know what to expect, but we all feared that Jesus's wine would never be replaced.

My wine soured twice as much, since I had lost both Jesus and Clopas. Like Martha, I tasted ashes as the two most important people in my life became dead to me. I cried out to God in anger. I couldn't believe that God would deliver unto me the joy of marriage and then abort it. Would all that Jesus went through with us be for nothing? No, to think such thoughts could lead me down a path I did not wish to go; a dark path, in which I could envision ending my own life. Before I could entertain this image further, I returned to the comfort of my new family.

For in them, I saw Jesus's idea of family. Family is more than one's kin or spouse; it is a community committed to following him together. My marriage, I thought, had fallen apart, just like my relationship with Martha had. But that didn't mean my world would fall apart, no matter what happened with Jesus. I was with them and that was what mattered. We'd drink the bitter wine together to ease our pain. We could tolerate the bitterness if we did it together.

CLOPAS: I ignored the pain I felt over Jesus's death and my rift with Mary by sharpening my sword and rehearsing my plan, punctuated by praying "Jesus, guide me." I think I slept some too. . . . It was an all-consuming experience, but I tried to block everything else out so I would be ready when Judas arrived early on Sunday morning.

Now, I had absorbed myself in the sharpening of one of the two 18-inch swords with the other to make it double-edged, just like Jesus had shown me. Then I strapped the sharp one to my right thigh under my garments. The other I held in my right hand, which might have been shaking, as I confronted Judas. He was surprised to see me. He taunted, "So Mary told you how to find the field? Good, now I can make her a widow. I'll send you to heaven, just like I did with Lazarus." I recognized his game. This was supposed to make me angry. So I pretended to be enraged. I charged him with my sword and when he knocked it out of my hand, like he had many times, he thought he had me. So I begged for my life, "Oh, Master Judas. . . ." It's what he expected of a peddler of words. But Jesus had made the word become flesh in me, so when he began to gloat, [motions] I grabbed his beard with my right hand. I stared briefly into his eyes and then decided to kiss him, as he had kissed Jesus. [Puckers but then, facing the crowd, laughs once with a downward inflection instead of following through.] As I did that, [Returns right hand into position and motions with left hand.] I reached with my left hand, took the sword from my right thigh, and plunged it up into Judas' belly with all my strength. Even the handle went in. [leans forward] Judas fell backwards, head-first and [spreads hands apart] burst open in the middle, and all his insides spilled out.[133] [hands on face, eyes cast downward] His blood spilled out onto me as I fell with him.

When I hit the ground, it was as if I awoke from the hazy trance of my preparation for this moment. Now free from suppression, all of my senses were suddenly screaming. There were pieces of Judas's intestines on my fingers and stuck to my robe. Some of his blood had spurted onto my lips. Inadvertently, I tasted that blood, cloying and metallic on my tongue. I hadn't anticipated the gore of killing someone. The sound, smell, taste, feel, and sight of Judas's death will forever remain with me. But I don't . . .I don't like to describe it beyond that. I don't . . . deserve to suffer . . . again for my sin. This part of the story is akin to a flogging, and the memory bears such acrid fruit.

---

[133] Judges 3:16-22, 2 Samuel 20:8-10, Acts 1:18

MARY: [She looks compassionately at him.] *We share those feelings in regards to the details of death. I don't like to speak much about Jesus's suffering on Good Friday. It's gruesome, not good news! We are telling people the good news!*

CLOPAS: Stumbling away from Judas, stained by blood, I lost whatever bit of food I'd had in my stomach. He lay there like a butchered animal, and the experience threatened to tear me apart. My feet were slick with blood, and I tripped, falling face down in the grass. Before I realized what I was doing, I began to chew the blades of grass that had made their way into my open mouth, slowly at first, but then in a frantic frenzy. When I slowed down to think about what I was doing, I felt like Nebuchadnezzar in the book of Daniel[134], but I don't think I was insane. I ate grass to remove the taste of Judas from my mouth and to distract . . . to dull my mind from . . . from everything. I felt my old self charging me, an insidious voice that told me to throw myself from a cliff. I rolled away from what had become a "field of blood" and toward a nearby cliff, my inward struggle raging. I scrubbed my clothes, my body, and my tongue with

---

[134] Daniel 4:33

dirt, grass, anything to blot out my
rebellion, to wash away my guilt, to
cleanse me from my sin[135]. I *hated* what
had happened so much that if I had had
hyssop, I would have purified myself;
I felt bad down to the marrow of my
bones[136]. [One arm held crossed horizontally over
stomach with the other arm's elbow pinning the hand
and holding up a clenched fist to within his mouth.]

But then, [removes fist from mouth and holds
hands open forward] then the words of my
prayer "Jesus, guide me!" [motions outward
with hands from head] thundered in my mind
and [clasps hands together] echoed through my
being. Then, as my warring parts [looks
upward and around] were distracted, [Mary
comes up behind Clopas to enact his words] it felt
like Jesus came up behind me and with
one arm, firmly hugged me, pulling me
away from the cliff, while with the
other he inserted what felt like a
horse's bit into my mouth. [She puts her
hand over his mouth for a moment and then steps
back.]

There'd been something missing,
something that had been shaken off by
my unholy focus and reverse-baptism of
blood. I turned completely away from
the remains of Judas and what had been

---

[135] **Psalm 51:1b-2**

[136] **Psalm 51:7**

wrought. [turns around once]

[holds out hands and looks down] I looked and saw that my hands, like the rest of me, were dirty. They were as dirty as they were after Jesus first gave me sight. They looked terribly dirty, but they didn't feel terribly guilty. On the inside, at least, I felt clean again, worthy of Jesus . . . and Mary. The thought of her caused me to run, and I darted off to find her. And, thank God, I didn't tell anyone else about Judas. For soon all of Jerusalem knew that Judas had met his demise in his field of blood[137].

MARY: *They knew he died but not how. We let them believe a story later made up by the chief priests and elders that Judas had felt remorse and taken his own life[138]. It's what we wished had happened . . . and it doesn't give any glory to violence.*

CLOPAS: Nobody should die because of Jesus's death on the cross. As David said to Saul, "Wickedness comes from wicked people. My hand will never be against you."[139] I wish that had been true. [sniffs] I should have been there at the cross with Mary.

MARY: [comforts Clopas] *Remember what David did*

---

[137] Acts 1:19

[138] Matthew 27:3-7

[139] 1 Samuel 24:12-15

when the baby that Uriah's wife had born to him became
ill. He at first refused all comfort. But when the baby
died, he rose up, worshipped the Lord and went on[140].
[Pause, Clopas steps back and Mary steps forward.]

---

[140] **2 Samuel 12:15-23**

On the Road to Emmaus

MARY: *We went on . . . which is what we intended to do after we anointed Jesus very early on Sunday. Most of us came to the tomb, but not the mother of Jesus, she remained too grief-stricken. We came bringing the spices we had prepared. We wanted to anoint him, worship, and move on with our lives together.*

CLOPAS: But when they arrived they found the stone rolled away from the tomb.

MARY: *We went in but did not find the body of the Lord Jesus. This perplexed us[141].*

CLOPAS: Suddenly, two men stood by them in dazzling clothes.

MARY: *I was terrified, as were the others. The only thing we could do was bow down to the ground[142].*

CLOPAS: [over-dramatic angel voice] "Why are you looking for the living among the dead?" asked the men. "He is not here, but he has been resurrected! Remember how he spoke to you when he was still in Galilee, saying 'The Son of Man must be betrayed into the hands of sinful men, be crucified, and rise on the third day?'"

MARY: *I remembered this but I didn't know what to*

---

[141] Luke 24:1-3

[142] Luke 24:4-5

believe. It filled me with trembling and astonishment[143]. I ran back to my family, my sorrow turning into anticipation. We reported all these things and more to the eleven apostles and to all the rest[144].

CLOPAS: I was part of "all the rest." I had recently arrived, and fortunately, the arrival of Mary Magdalene, Joanna, Mary, and other women kept me from getting much attention with my soiled clothing and tale of Judas's death. The women were so excited they could barely contain themselves. But their words seemed like nonsense to us. We did not believe them[145]. They all tried to talk at once, disagreeing on huge details, but it was clear that they said Jesus's body was not in his tomb.

MARY: *It was discouraging how quickly our familial bonds turned resentful as we each tried to describe what we'd seen at the tomb. All of the women who'd been there grew angry with each other, trying to convince one another that what they'd seen was the truth. Then we resented that our differing accounts cast doubt amongst the men. I don't know why our accounts differed so much. I just know that it was a fantastic moment, and we were all sincere about what we saw, even if we painted it differently with our different minds.*

CLOPAS: I saw Mary believed it, but

---

[143] **Mark 16:8**

[144] **Luke 24:6-9**

[145] **Luke 24:10**

like her and everyone else, I didn't
know what that meant. When our eyes
finally met, I watched as hers grew
wide with surprise. But right then
Peter and John got up and ran away.

MARY: *They were at least willing to go see it for themselves. I don't blame people for not believing us. I wouldn't have believed us. We didn't know what to believe. As Mary Magdalene cried out, "They have taken the Lord out of the tomb, and we don't know where they have put him!*[146]*" It didn't make any sense, why take Jesus away? But if he'd been resurrected then why were the linen cloths they wrapped him in lying in the tomb? Why wasn't he there or nearby if he'd been resurrected? It wasn't the way things happened for my brother.*

It was one mystery after another, first Jesus disappearing and now Clopas reappearing. If I had been calmer, perhaps I might have seen the truth. But after my anointing of Jesus with my whole dowry, loss of my sister Martha, engagement to Clopas, death of Lazarus, first fight with Clopas, two-day preparations for our wedding, second fight with Clopas, and the rest of the drama of the crucifixion of Jesus, all in the last week, I'm glad I didn't faint when I saw Clopas! I wondered, "When would the troubled waters of my soul be calmed?"

CLOPAS: We were sheep with no shepherd.
Although we should have known better,
Jesus's betrayal by Judas and
crucifixion had caught us by surprise.

---

[146] John 20:2

He'd always managed to escape all the close calls we'd been through. And, as with Lazarus, the thought of Jesus's resurrection went against everything that made sense. How could he resurrect himself, especially after such a gruesome death? But if it were true then so what? Where was he and what would that mean for us? It was hard to ponder those questions with so little sleep, and we were already divided over other more immediate worries.

MARY: *Some were afraid that Judas would lead the authorities to find us next.*

CLOPAS: Others weren't afraid of the authorities. Jesus had *not* declared a successor. The obvious consequence was that they knew we were no threat to anyone. Without a head, we would fall apart. Thus, we had to set up a new "Way," which reopened the old, painful argument of attempting to decide who was the greatest among the apostles.

MARY: *Never mind that they took for granted that the women supporters of Jesus would continue to support them. . . . There was a reason our earlier focus had been on the anointment of Jesus.*

CLOPAS: Our disagreements multiplied, not unlike how things had gone between Mary and I after Jesus cleansed the temple. I caught the end of the debate when I arrived. I didn't miss anything. They were stuck going back and forth.

They didn't even give me a chance to say what I had to say. It was like I was nobody again; [sarcastically] there's no way I could have had anything to contribute. . . .

But when Peter and John distracted everyone by jumping up and running away, the fighting died down. Everyone remained together; where else could we go? Despite the crowded space, I pushed my way to Mary and kissed her.

MARY: *The kiss was not unwelcome, but it was an awkward moment. It was difficult to separate myself and my emotions from all that had happened and just be present with Clopas. Mary Magdalene wanted to go back to the tomb. The rest of the women declined. It seemed a pointless task since no one would believe us anyhow. So, Mary Magdalene went alone. Clopas and I went aside to talk. I spoke first. "I thought you were dead. I thought I had lost both Jesus and you. I don't care what happened, and I don't care about Judas, I missed you so. Don't ever do that to me again!"*

CLOPAS: I stammered a similar response and then we kissed and embraced again. She asked about my clothes, and I told her I'd explain everything later. Soon, Peter and John returned with the news that the tomb indeed was empty, but by then we agreed it was time for us to go to Emmaus.

MARY: *We needed to go on. Neither of us wanted any part in the heated debates, or infighting over who was the greatest apostle. We agreed that only one thing was necessary: for us to remain together. Our relationship had been through so much in the past week. . . . Our bond had been bent and warped, twice almost broken forever. Unlike Jesus's crucifixion and possible resurrection, we thought our marriage was something we could maybe do something about.*

CLOPAS: So we said some goodbyes. We didn't say goodbye for forever, but it kind of felt like that. . . . Mary Magdalene had not returned yet, but we didn't wait for her.

MARY: *Thanks to her, our* [sighs] *"honeymoon" was all set, except the wine of our joy had been drained dry. Too many tears turned wine into vinegar. Jesus had died, and his tomb was empty, but we were lost. My husband who had died to me had returned, but we were still lost. Without Jesus, how could I trust Clopas? I thought Jesus had led him to turn away from the way of the Zealot for good. But then he went right back to it and away from me when I needed him most.*

I hadn't shared anything about Clopas with the other women on Good Friday. I could only stammer that he was gone. It felt shameful to mention his delusion and our fight while Jesus was being tortured and crucified. But, in a way, it also felt like our troubles were on that cross as well. We had been a new couple, a new reality that Jesus made possible and we fell apart, just like that. . . .

And, Clopas's return didn't heal my wounds. He was still Clopas being Clopas; he didn't understand how deeply his quest had wounded me, exacerbating the pain of watching Jesus die on the cross. Without Jesus to center us, we were angrier and more frustrated. And it just grew worse as we tried to discuss how we would support ourselves, which is probably the least desirable question for "honeymooners" to deal with. . . .

CLOPAS: All our hopes had become tied up with the followers of Jesus and who knew how long that would last?

I was also wounded, for as disgusted as I was with Judas's death, I still felt God's hand in my deliverance. And, it hurt that Mary didn't even try to see from my vantage point as I told her the whole tale of how Judas met his end. She refused to recognize that God had inspired me with stories from the Torah. The left-handed judge Ehud had slain Eglon, the fat king of the Moabites,[147] and David's general Joab had slain his rival Amasa[148] in a similar manner to the way I'd chosen to end Judas's life. Murder was murder to Mary, plain and simple. I could see

---

[147] Judges 3:16-22

[148] 2 Samuels 20:8-10

that she was consumed by the pain of being left in the shadow of the cross, without hope for us.

And it was hard for me to see then that I might've been exalting myself in killing Judas. Part of me still wanted to win our previous fight, and so I turned away from the horror of killing a man.

MARY: *It's only seven miles to Emmaus, but we walked so slowly. The trip had begun to feel like our marriage did. Not knowing where else to go, or what to do, we just kept walking.*

CLOPAS: Our old fears and anxieties rose to the surface. We'd been on an emotional roller coaster ride, and we found ourselves arguing about Jesus and politics, Judas, and Jesus's teachings and . . . and it was dreadful. There was a lot of heat and little light, probably because our real questions were too painful to ask. Was this all a mistake?

MARY: *Why did Jesus make such a mismatch of us?*

CLOPAS AND MARY: **How could he be so wrong about our match, and be crucified, if he were the true Messiah?**

[Silence.]

MARY: *And then the desire to survive shut down all other emotions. We weren't late. The plan had been to* travel to Emmaus on Sunday, but we were sure Mary Magdalene's contacts in Emmaus had heard about the crucifixion of Jesus.

CLOPAS: Besides, we didn't want to return to Jerusalem. At least not for awhile. . . . The memories were too painful and the conflicts within the followers of Jesus were discouraging. We both felt unsafe. We needed a sanctuary.

MARY: It was the only hope for us. We needed our own supporters to give us the time to breath and decide together how to follow Jesus.

CLOPAS: But that meant we needed to work together to succeed in what we had both failed at: to tell our stories to win supporters for Jesus.

MARY: But first we had to explain to them what had happened on the morning of the empty tomb. We needed to make sense of it so that they'd understand and want us to stay with them longer than the original plan.

CLOPAS: The most important thing in our telling was how to hook them, to begin the story as simply as possible so that they wanted to hear more. We couldn't mention all the competing details of the different accounts of what happened at Jesus's tomb that morning. We had to boil things down, just like Jesus did with his parables.

MARY: This wasn't too hard to do. We agreed to cover

the facts and to minimize our role in the events. It's the same thing we do most of the time when we give our performance of the good news. What was more difficult was where to go from there. How long should we stay in Emmaus? Where would we go next?

CLOPAS: Fortunately, we then realized we had the model of Jesus sending out pairs of disciples to the towns where he planned to visit[149]. With God's help, this would sustain us.

MARY: But we didn't know what message we'd share or if anyone would still want to hear about Jesus. It was kind of a blessing to get caught up in discussing everything that had taken place[150], for it distracted us from our problems. And while we were discussing—

CLOPAS: and arguing.

MARY: Yes, while we were discussing and arguing, Jesus himself came near and began to walk along with us[151].

CLOPAS: But our eyes were prevented from recognizing him. Then he asked,

MARY: "What are these words you are exchanging with each other as you walk?" And so we stopped. I wondered: did we sound that bad? Even a stranger had noticed our tone! How were we going to persuade anyone to support us if we couldn't agree on a common story? But this "fellow" was a chance to practice, which we definitely

---

[149] Luke 10:1-5

[150] Luke 24:14

[151] Luke 24:15

needed.

CLOPAS: The opportunity to practice our pitch was communicated nonverbally; it must've been hard for Jesus not to laugh at it. I swallowed and began, "Are you the only visitor in Jerusalem who doesn't know the things that happened there in these days?[152]"

MARY: *"What things?" Jesus asked.*

"The things concerning Jesus the Nazarene."

CLOPAS: "Who was a prophet powerful in action and speech before God and all the people."

MARY: *"Our chief priests and leaders handed him over to be sentenced to death, and they crucified him."*

CLOPAS AND MARY: ***"But we were hoping that he was the one who was about to redeem Israel."***

MARY: *"Besides all this, it's the third day since these things happened."*

CLOPAS: "Moreover, some women from our group astonished us."

MARY: *"They arrived early at the tomb, and when they didn't find his body, they came and reported that they had seen a vision of angels who said he was alive."*

CLOPAS: "Some of those who were with us went to the tomb and found it just as

---

[152] Luke 24:18

the women had said, but they didn't see him.[153]"

MARY: *It was our first performance. It just wasn't quite good or good news yet. Then Jesus said to us, "how unwise and slow you are to believe in your hearts all that the prophets have spoken! Didn't the Messiah have to suffer these things and enter into his glory?*[154]"

CLOPAS: We still had no clue it was him. Then beginning with Moses and all the prophets, he interpreted the things concerning himself in all the Scriptures[155].

MARY: *He did this as well as could be imagined, but it was an overwhelming amount. I felt like I had fallen into a pond that was deeper than the oceans. And in what felt like minutes, we came near the village where we were going.*

CLOPAS: Jesus gave the impression that he was going farther, but there was no way we were going to let him leave us without more explanations. We couldn't kidnap him, so we did the next best thing. We urged him, "Stay with us, because it's almost evening and now the day is almost over.[156]"

MARY: *This was close to true, but it was also just a*

---

[153] Luke 24:19-24

[154] Luke 24:25-26

[155] Luke 24: 27

[156] Luke 24:29

polite way of attempting to persuade him to stay with us. All our plans and words though were as worthless as straw. My mind was like an over-full belly. I cannot remember what we said and did next, but we must've arrived at our destination. It's all lost in the shadow of how Jesus was revealed to us.

CLOPAS: The next thing I remember, it seemed as if Jesus reclined at the table with us, and he took the bread, blessed and broke it, and gave it to us. Then our eyes were opened, and it felt like second sight. We recognized him,

MARY: *but he disappeared from our sight[157]. Yes, he disappeared!*

CLOPAS: So we said to each other,

MARY AND CLOPAS: ***"Weren't our hearts ablaze within us while he was talking with us on the road and explaining the Scriptures to us?" That very hour we got up and returned to Jerusalem[158].***

CLOPAS: We journeyed quickly, not too unlike my trip to find Jesus and save Lazarus, except this time, we were together, overcome in unbelievable joy. "Jesus has been raised!" we chanted all the way to where we found the Eleven and those with them. All

---

[157] Luke 24:30-31

[158] Luke 24:32-33a

those gathered together said "The Lord has certainly been raised, and has appeared to Simon![159]"

MARY: *But Thomas excused himself before we began to describe what had happened on the road and how he was made known to us in the breaking of the bread[160].*

CLOPAS: It would have been our second try to tell the story of Jesus and us, but as we were saying these things, Jesus himself stood among us. He said,

MARY: *"Peace to you![161]"* [Laughing] *Which was exactly the opposite of what occurred! We were startled and terrified. Were we seeing a ghost[162]?*

CLOPAS: [imitates Jesus] "Why are you troubled? And why do doubts arise in your hearts? Look at my hands and my feet, that it is I myself! Touch me and see, because a ghost does not have flesh and bones as you can see I have." Having said this, he showed us his hands and feet.

MARY: *But while we still were amazed and unbelieving, he asked us, "Do you have anything here to eat?" So we gave him a piece of a broiled fish and some honeycomb, and he took it and ate in our presence[163].*

---

[159] Luke 24:33b-34

[160] Luke 24:35

[161] Luke 24:36

[162] Luke 24:37

[163] Luke 24: 41-43

While he was eating, Clopas and I went to speak with him. We thanked him for coming to us on the road to Emmaus. We apologized for not remembering what he told us.

CLOPAS: I didn't say it, but it seemed like he had chosen the wrong people to share with. Jesus sensed our shame and said,

MARY: *"Mary and Clopas, you two together have become a well from which will pour forth much living water! What I shared with you, it is all there inside your well. When you have need of it, parts will rise to the surface and be recognized by how it sets your hearts ablaze again. But I hear your concern."*

CLOPAS: He addressed us as a group again, "These are my words that I spoke to you while I was still with you—that everything written about me in the Law of Moses, the Prophets, and the Psalms must be fulfilled." Then he opened our minds yet again to understand the Scriptures[164]. And yet again, the whole truth was too heavy for us, though it did set our hearts ablaze.

MARY: *He also said, "this is what is written: the Messiah would suffer and rise from the dead the third day, and repentance for forgiveness of sins would be proclaimed in his name to all the nations, beginning at*

---

[164] Luke 24: 44-45

Jerusalem. You are witnesses of these things."

CLOPAS: He sensed our anxiety over the weight of the gift he had given us all. "And look, I am sending upon you what my Father promised. As for you, stay in the city until you are clothed with power from on high." [165]

MARY: *Jesus said again, "Peace to you! As the Father has sent me, I also send you." After saying this, he breathed and said to us, "Receive the Holy Spirit. If you forgive the sins of any, they are forgiven them; if you retain the sins of any, they are retained." [166] When he said this, it felt like he was looking at us. Amazingly, we both remembered at the same time his words from before we went to Jerusalem.*

CLOPAS: "It is impossible for causes of stumbling not to come. . . .

MARY: *If your brother sins, rebuke him,*

CLOPAS AND MARY: **and if he repents, forgive him.** [167] **"**

CLOPAS: Had I repented of leaving Mary in the shadow of the cross?

MARY: *Had I forgiven Clopas for the murder of Judas?*

CLOPAS: Our eyes met. What many words had failed to do was accomplished without words in a matter of seconds.

---

[165] Luke 24: 46-49

[166] John 20:21-23

[167] Luke 17:1, 3a

I apologized.

MARY: *I forgave.*

CLOPAS: With Jesus's help, we did what hours of discussion on the road to Emmaus had failed to do.

MARY: *We became Jesus and us, once more.*

CLOPAS: Then, Jesus disappeared again.

MARY: *Everyone was exhausted and the wave of fatigue was tenfold compared to Lazarus's resurrection. It's like God had granted us the energy we needed to keep awake while Jesus was with us, but now that he had gone, everyone was ready to sleep right then and there.*

CLOPAS: Well, not all of us were ready to sleep. [Laughs] As I gazed on the wife who I love, I remembered tonight was supposed to be our honeymoon night and felt God stirring my loins with another blessing.

MARY: [Laughs] *Yes, indeed!*

A Blessed Beginning and Ending to Our Story

MARY: *In the evening of the next day, we had another meeting. There were three matters that needed to be discussed. First, Mary Magdalene let us know that she had taken the spices and perfumes we had prepared for Jesus[168], and sold them for enough to provide for us all for a month. These spices hadn't been dropped!* [laughs] *She assured us we need not worry about money. When there was need, Joseph of Arimathea and others would provide again. And, this time, we agreed, at the suggestion of the mother of Jesus, who'd just made public her commitment to persuading her children of the flesh to become her brothers and sisters of the spirit, that Mary Magdalene would tend the common purse on behalf of us all!*

CLOPAS: Second, it seemed to some that Jesus had contradicted himself. For last night, he told us to stay in the city. During his last supper, he had promised, "But after I have been resurrected, I will go ahead of you to Galilee.[169]" This prophecy had been confirmed by angelic prophecy at Jesus's tomb that Jesus would be going ahead to Galilee and that we would see him there.[170]

---

[168] Luke 23:56

[169] Matthew 26:32, Mark 14:28

[170] Matthew 28:7, Mark 16:7

MARY: *So did we obey Jesus by staying in the city or did we obey his prophecy to meet us in Galilee? We prayed some and Peter declared that the Eleven would split between Jerusalem and Galilee. Nathanael suggested his step-father's residence in Cana was a good place to stay.*

CLOPAS: But this brought up the third issue; what to do about Thomas? He had not returned yet. The ten apostles all agreed that they first had to reconcile with Thomas before any of them went to Galilee.

MARY: *Like Peter said, "It's what Jesus wants, for us all to be brothers . . . and sisters."*

CLOPAS: But Nathanael wanted someone to go ahead to Cana right then. They would prepare a place for them. We volunteered. This made sense to everyone.

MARY: *After all, we hadn't exactly had our honeymoon yet and, more importantly, after our encounter with Jesus on the road to Emmaus, they trusted us to tell the story of Jesus and us. So the next day we worked it out and set off to Cana on foot together. Along the way, we discussed how we would tell the good news this time.*

CLOPAS: And, the third time was the charm. Nathanael's two families wept for joy with us over the good news we had shared with them.

MARY: *Then we shared more of our own stories with them, including the stories of our wedding with Jesus, as they shared with us stories of their wedding with Jesus. We soon came to regard each other as family. And they blessed us with a wonderful honeymoon!*

CLOPAS: It was unforgettable, well only "forgettable" in the shadow of the cross. All aspects of our own story can be forgotten or told only as they contribute to the story of Jesus.

Then, within a week or so, we were joined by Peter, a believing Thomas, Nathanael, and the sons of Zebedee.[171]

MARY: *It was a joyful reunion, and soon Peter and Nathanael got to see their wives. And then we waited . . .*

CLOPAS: and waited . . . for weeks. Finally, Simon Peter said, "I'm going fishing."

MARY: *We all told him we were coming with him and went out and got into the boat. This was a frightening prospect since neither Clopas nor I had been in a boat before, much less fished. That night Clopas threw up three times, and we caught nothing.[172]*

CLOPAS: They offered to take me back, but I insisted that we continue. When daybreak came, Jesus stood on the shore. However, once again we could not tell that it was Jesus.[173] Part of it was the distance, but the other part

---

[171] John 21:2

[172] John 21: 3

[173] John 21:4

of it was Jesus's new way of being. He showed us only what he wanted to show us of himself.

MARY: *"Children," Jesus called to us. "You don't have any fish, do you?" We answered, "No."*

"Cast the net on the right side of the boat," he told us. "And you'll find some."

CLOPAS: So we cast out our net, and we were unable to haul it in because of the large number of fish. At this, John said to Peter, "It is the Lord!"

MARY: *When Simon Peter heard that it was the Lord, he tied his outer garment around him*

CLOPAS: [interrupting] for he was stripped,

MARY: [continuing] *and plunged into the sea. But since we were not far from land, the rest of us came in the boat, dragging the net full of fish. When we got out on land, we saw a charcoal fire there, with fish lying on it, and bread.*

CLOPAS: "Bring some of the fish you've just caught," Jesus told us. We were all in shock so Peter got up and got so excited that he hauled the net ashore, full of large fish. It was a Samson-like feat; when we counted the fish, they were 153 in number. And, even though there were so many, the net was not torn[174]. It was a miracle it

---

[174] John 21:6-11

was ready to catch more. There was just one miracle after another. . . .

MARY: Then Jesus broke our stupor by telling us to, "come and have breakfast." We obeyed but we remained silent. None of us dared ask him, "who are you?" because we knew it was the Lord. We just still didn't quite believe it yet.

CLOPAS: Once again, our instincts betrayed what we knew in our hearts. Jesus came, took the bread, and gave it to us. He did the same with the fish.[175]

CLOPAS AND MARY: *It wasn't quite the same as before, Jesus felt different to us. But this was our third and last time we personally interacted with Jesus and like before, it changed our lives forever.*

CLOPAS: Immediately after breakfast, Jesus spent time with Peter walking and talking on the beach, with John following them.

MARY: *It was an important conversation that we often do tell, but not this time. . . .*

CLOPAS: For there were also many other things that Jesus did,

MARY: *so many that if they were written one by one,*

CLOPAS: I suppose not even the world

---

[175] John 21:13

itself could contain the scroll that would be written[176].

MARY AND CLOPAS: *But soon Jesus answered the question on both of our hearts: "Why us?"* [pause]

MARY AND CLOPAS: [Jesus voices together] *"Do you remember the prophecy of Hosea? When we, my father and I through our spirit of Truth, first spoke to Hosea, we told him to go and marry a promiscuous wife and have children of promiscuity. We said this so he could testify about how Israel was committing blatant acts of promiscuity by abandoning us[177]. We needed his heart to break so he could show the house of Israel how painful their rebellion was to us.*

When your sufferings came about, we saw that our works could be displayed in your story. We saw how much love you both needed and deserved. We saw how easily you'd go astray, even after Jesus saved each of you. This made you our new Hosea and Gomer, the couple who fits their time and age. For you are a sign for our new Israel. Your families and dreams had to crumble so together, you could represent our new family. You are an unlikely couple, and your relationship will be full of difficulties, as you continue to be different. But through us, how we are present in your differences, you will

---

[176] John 21:25

[177] Hosea 1:2

find strength and the power to heal your wounds. A healing balm will spring up from deep in your souls and spill over to heal many.

This is why you have found favor with us.

Mary, you have conceived and will give birth to a son, and you must not call his name Jesus!

Instead, you will call him James, the younger[178].*

For he will be part of my new family!

You will do the same with the names of all your sons and daughters.

They must share the names of Jesus's half-brothers and half-sisters, for they represent our blessing on you both and how you together will increase our flock.

[silence]

CLOPAS AND MARY: *With that we began our new reality, which has blessed us with many chances to share the story of Jesus. Like we said before, we normally do not share so much of our part in the story.*

CLOPAS: We also prefer to gloss over small details like how Jesus was short

MARY: *but fit.*

MARY AND CLOPAS: *We do this, because we don't want anything to distract you from the*

---

[178] Mark 15:40

good news. The same is true of much of our stories.

And so if we ever were to contribute part of our performances to be written down, it would be best for them to only hint at our story. The story of Jesus and us would remain a love story in the shadow of the cross; where it belongs.

CLOPAS: As for us, we both kept changing. . . .

MARY: *I became a wife and a mother.*

CLOPAS: I saw that every time we say, "Christ is Lord," we also say, "Caesar is not Lord!" This statement is more powerful for me because I believe it's possible that Jesus could have been Caesar.

MARY: *But he would have had to sacrifice the lives of many of his followers in the process. Those like Mary Magdalene or Peter . . . or* [motions to Clopas] *you and me.*

CLOPAS: It seems as if he chose us, and I wonder, were we worth it? Can the world truly be changed by the telling of this story? I trust that our sharing what Jesus has shared with us will transform this world in ways we cannot even imagine.

MARY: *I accepted that the risk of martyrdom is part of taking up our crosses to follow Jesus. If Clopas or I fall* into the death of a martyr, then I trust the living Christ will bless the remaining one of us to continue on with our new family.

MARY AND CLOPAS: *And we will be together again, as truly brother and sister in Christ some day!*

~ ~ ~ ~ ~

Acknowledgements

For the "Marys of Magdalene" and "Josephs of Arimathea"or the major backers of **The Story of Jesus and Us** —

THANK YOU SO VERY MUCH!

David E. and Connie Wetzell, *my friends and my parents*

Enrique de la Rosa, *my friend and former student*

David Hovde, *my friend and mentor*

Philip "Pip" Rhoads, *my friend and printer extraordinaire*

Joseph Marshak, *my friend and author of the first draft of the wedding and passover scenes*

Bridgette Lewis, *my friend and marketing consultant*

"God's Child" (Anonymous), *my friend*

Bob Lembke, *my friend and inspiration for Lazarus*

Christina Walker, *my friend and sister/ encourager extraordinaire*

Made in the USA
Charleston, SC
10 November 2012